Tragedy of The Heart

Dedication

This book was written with love for my mom.

Thanking Reilly Perry (Perry Productions Inc.) for helping with the creation of the cover. It was a pleasure meeting and working with you.

INTRODUCTION

Back in the day, people used to want their children's skin to be exceptionally light so they could take advantage of good job opportunities when they grew up. They felt if you were born too dark, others would look down on you and offer you bottom-of-the-barrel jobs.

There was a girl born into a family of seven children (*4 boys and 3 girls*) in the late 1940s and 50s. She was number five of the bunch. Her name was Catherine. She was considered the darkest child of the bunch. The other children were called high yellow.

Mother was beautiful, her skin color was high yellow, and she had long jet black/wavy hair ((*like Indian hair*)). She stood about 5'9, with the body of a high paid model. But she had the attitude of the wicked. The way she acted, and thought would send chills through anyone.

Father was what some would call handsome. His skin color was caramel, and his hair was black, short, and curly. He stood about 6'0, with the body of a stocky guy.

He was a hard worker and tried to make sure his family was taken care of. He was a firm and loving father and husband and expected things to be done in order around the house while he was at work. He was sweet in his own way but did not seem to exercise self-control when it came down to his wife.

Bernadette the baby sister of the bunch, skin was high yellow like her mom. She was a little taller than Catherine with hair like regular black folks (*soft but nappy*). She envied Catherine to the point that jealously showed its ugly head. The envy was fed by the negativity radiating from mother.

Bernadette always tried to portray herself as the innocent one, but in her heart, she was always scheming to get over on somebody. She always got away with murder, because it was easy to blame things on Catherine (*mother would always believe the worst regarding her*).

Catherine was just light skinned (*if you call that a big difference*). So, I guess she was almost the color of her father. She was beautiful and had beautiful long black, wavy hair (*like Indian hair*) and stood about 5'2. She was smart as a whip and had sassiness about her.

Tabatha the eldest sister was high yellow, stood about the same height as mother. Her hair texture was the same as the youngest sister.

Tabatha had an extraordinary mean streak. She did not like anyone and wanted everything to be about her. She also developed jealousy tendencies towards Catherine.

Every time they went outside someone would pay Catherine a compliment, which angered Tabatha.

She was tired of hearing all the compliments toward Catherine. She felt that she was the better looking one, because she had high yellow skin. She always felt her presence was mightier than the other sisters. She just could not understand what it was about Catherine that drew the boys/men to her.

Tabatha decided she was going to make her mark one way or the other. Any opportunity she saw to get Catherine in trouble she took (*it never took much to persuade mother to go against her*).

George the baby of the bunch, skin color was in between the color of mother and Catherine. He was also blessed with the same texture of hair as baby sister. He was a frail little thing that kept to himself most of the time.

He did not have a clear understanding of the things going on around him at the time, but he listened to Bernadette a lot when it came to getting Catherine in trouble.

Mark was the clown of the bunch. His skin color and hair texture were the same as George. He stood about 5'7 and had a stocky build.

Mark loved playing jokes on people and pissing people off. He fed on other people's aggravation; the more you got mad at him the more he would do.

He did not care too much about anything. He felt like what was, was what it is. He thought his family was full of a bunch of fools and plotted the first chance he got he was going to get away from them.

Guy was the dreamer of the bunch. He looked just like George and Mark. His height was the only difference between them. He stood around the same height as mother and Tabatha, just a wee bit taller and slender. He always had his head up in the cloud.

He always thought about leaving home, because he was ashamed to be a part of the family.

Guy vowed to get away from everyone when he was older. He did not want to live like they were living any longer and knew his chance was going to come one day.

Jermaine the oldest of the bunch was also high yellow skinned with regular black hair like his siblings. He was taller than everyone. He stood about 6'0 tall and had a thin strong physique.

When mom was drunk and unable to function as a parent, Jermaine stepped up and took on the responsibilities. He cooked, cleaned, and became the disciplinary. He started to resent his mother because of all the responsibilities he had to take on due to her drunkenness.

Jermaine's feelings were unlike the other siblings; **he despised Catherine**.

Every time he went outside someone would ask him about her. He grew tired of hearing her name.

Every time he saw her, something in him would make him pick at her. What started off as constant arguing suddenly became physical; *they fought constantly*.

No one in the family understood where all the hatred came from.

Although he appeared the more masculine of the brothers and stronger than the rest, later the world would come to know of his hidden feminine tendencies.

CHAPTER 1

Father loved his family dearly and only wanted the best for them and worked hard to provide that.

The children rarely saw him because he worked all the time. By the time he got home from work, the children were in bed. The only time he and mother spent time together was at the dinner table and bed.

Mother always made sure that father's dinner was ready when he arrived home. After dinner, he took a bath and went to bed. This was the routine for years.

As the children grew, mother became restless. After cleaning the house and getting the children off to school, she had nothing to do.

Mother tried to address the problems with father, but that always led to arguments.

She grew tired of the situation and began drinking. First, it was from time to time, but as time went on, she began to drink more and more.

This began to cause huge problems between mother and father.

Mother did not work, so she had no money to support her habit. She started using the grocery money that father left to drink with.

This made the house short of food quite often.

While going to the store for her binges, she began meeting men. They loved the way that she looked, and she loved the attention. So, she began entertaining them with conversation.

Mother stopped having dinner ready when father got home and the house was not always clean, like it used to be. The children were still in bed by the time their father got home, but they went to bed with empty stomachs most of the time.

Mother and Father began to have severe domestic problems when Catherine and her sibling were growing up. Throughout the marriage, mother continued to drink and stray.

CHAPTER 2

The whole neighborhood started gossiping about the things that they saw mother doing.

The neighbor's began telling father about the activities going on at the house, while he was at work.

He could not believe what he was hearing; the news made his heart drop down to the bottom of his stomach.

Father decided not to take the neighbors at their word and find out for himself.

One day father decided to get off work early to see if what he was told was true (*He did not let his wife know of his decision*).

When he arrived at the house, he decided to hide where no one could see him. But he wanted to make sure he could see everything from where he was standing. So, he hid in between a couple of buildings with a clear view of where he lived.

It did not take long for him to see some activity going on at the apartment (*he was shocked by what he saw*).

Mother was up to her same routine. She made sure the children got out for school on time and once they left, one of her strays began coming up the stairs.

Once the gentleman arrived at the top of the stairs, mother greeted him with a hug and kiss, and proceeded to enter the apartment.

Father could not believe his eyes as he watched from across the street.

He saw this guy climb the stairs to their apartment. He saw his wife open the door with a gown on and welcome the man inside with a bright smile.

CHAPTER 3

He didn't know what to do; his legs were stuck in place and there was so much pain in his chest.

He didn't know what was going on with his body, but he knew he had to get it together.

A few moments passed as he felt his anger stirring. He felt as though he was going to kill somebody.

He ran up to the apartment and burst through the door. He saw the guy and his wife sitting close together on the couch (*both of their faces looked shocked and horrified*).

He yelled, "WHAT THE HELL IS GOING ON HERE!"

He grabbed the man and started punching him. The man started fighting back. They were crashing into everything. They nearly tore up the whole apartment (*all you could hear was rumbling and mother screaming*).

There was blood splattering everywhere (*the blood came from both*).

Father dominated the fight and ended up opening the door and throwing the man down the stairs.

The guy went tumbling down the stairs losing one of his shoes. He was trying to grab everything to stop himself from tumbling, but there was no stopping until he reached the bottom. He rolled over to get up while holding his head. He looked up at father and continued heading down the rest of the stairs, gathering himself.

People in the building began coming out of their apartments to see what was going on. They were shocked to see the guy at the bottom of the stairs bleeding and trying to get up. They looked up at the top of the stairs and saw father yelling.

Father screamed "DON'T EVER LET ME CATCH YOU OVER HERE AGAIN! IF I EVER SEE YOUR FACE AROUND HERE AGAIN, I WILL KILL YOU!"

No one went over to try to help the guy get up. They just looked at him and shook their heads in disbelief.

The man said nothing, he just got up and started walking fast while holding his head.

You know everyone in the neighborhood was going to be talking about this. Neither one of them would be able to live this situation down.

CHAPTER 4

Father turned away from the stairs of the porch and went inside. He closed the door and started in on his wife.

He beat her like she was a stranger from off the street. He was going in on her like he had lost his mind.

He beat her from the living room, all the way to the bedroom while yelling "YOU FILTHY BITCH, HOW COULD YOU HAVE THAT MAN IN MY HOUSE. I GO TO WORK AND THIS IS WHAT YOU DO TO ME. YOU FILTHY WHORE, I CAN'T BELIEVE YOU BROUGHT ANOTHER MAN IN MY HOUSE. I COULD KILL YOU RIGHT NOW! I SHOULD KILL YOU RIGHT NOW!"

Mother kept saying that she was sorry, but he would not let up. She was blocking the punches as much as she could, but there was nothing she could do to get him off her.

She protected herself as much she could by covering her face with her arms. But for the most part, all she could do is take it and pray that he stopped soon.

By the time father stopped beating her, she was butt ass naked and bloody from head to toe. He just looked at her while breathing heavily with his fists balled up. He opened his hands, rubbed his head, groaned, and walked away leaving the house.

CHAPTER 5

When the children arrived home, they saw blood all over the living room. They ran to their parent's room and saw their mom; She had black eyes, bruised arms, and a busted/bloodied head.

They were terrified and saddened by this sight.

The children put their things away and started taking care of their mother's wounds. They put witch hazel on her eyes and arms. They put a cold towel on her head and used another towel to clean the blood off.

While the older children continued to take care of mother, the rest made sure the house was clean and she ate like she was supposed to.

Father came back in the house, saying nothing. He just looked at the kids, held his head down and walked towards the bedroom.

The children looked at each other as their father walked past and decided to keep everything quiet so that they did not anger him.

CHAPTER 6

After the violent outburst from their dad against their mom was over, things calmed down for a while, or at least until mother healed.

After the healing process took place, mother began to do what she loved to do.

The fighting started happening often.

Father started missing work more and more, trying to keep an eye on his wife. This made the family struggle more than usual.

Mother would not stop the things that she was doing. She wouldn't stop drinking and she would not stop entertaining other men in the home.

As the fighting continued, mother began moving us back and forth from grandmother's house to back home. We moved away from father many times, but mother would always bring us back home.

The last fight that we witnessed was life-changing; we thought father was going to kill mother.

Father caught mother with another man again. This time they were in the bedroom having sex.

When father opened the door and saw what was going on, he ran over to the bed to grab the man. The man jumped up, grabbed his clothes, and ran out the house before father could get a hold to him.

Father ended up grabbing mother and began punching her. He punched her on the right and left side of her face. He kicked her in the stomach continuously. He grabbed her by the hair and crashed her head into the wall repeatedly (*blood was splattering everywhere*).

We saw mother crawling on the floor, spitting up blood. Her face was bruised with green and purple marks. She was saying in a weak voice "no more, please no more."

Father was standing over her with sweat running down his face and his fists closed tightly. He was shouting "GET OUT, BEFORE I KILL YOU. YOU AIN'T NOTHING BUT A SLUT AND WHORE. GET OUT MY HOUSE, BEFORE I KILL YOU".

Mother got up looking sad and scared. She grabbed something to put on and told us to get our things as fast as we could because we were leaving.

That was the last time we saw our parents fight.

CHAPTER 7

Catherine's family moved in with their grandmother for a while after that. By the time Catherine reached eight years old, they moved into the newly built 14 level project building on the south side of Chicago. It was a four-bedroom, one-bath apartment.

When entering the apartment, the first thing that you saw was a long hall with a closet. You could see the spacious living room from the hall. When you get to the end of the hall, there is an opening where you turn a bit, and you can see the kitchen. The kitchen had white cabinets, a stove, and a refrigerator. It also had a nice pantry area to store food.

When you turned the opposite way, there was a longer hall where the bedrooms were. The bedrooms were very spacious. The bathroom was in the middle of the hall and everything in it was white. There was also a storage closet and shelving closet.

This apartment had a lot of space for the family to be comfortable.

These newly built projects had beautiful green grass growing all around them. It was beautiful and mother had high hopes for a new beginning.

The children loved to see their mother smile. Because when she's happy, everything usually goes well.

After a few months of being in this new environment, mother started to meet people. She socialized quite often, especially with men (*some married*). Then she began drinking again.

At first, it was social, then it became heavy, and the beating of the children began.

This is when everything started going downhill for Catherine.

CHAPTER 8

Mother started criticizing Catherine often. She started to strongly emphasize the darkness of her skin in a negative way.

Mother's actions made the children focus on it too. They saw the resentment that she had for Catherine and began to use it to their advantage.

Catherine and her siblings started having a hard time getting along. Everyone was tired of getting beaten by mother, so the siblings conspired against her.

They knew mother always showed a bit of favoritism towards them because they were lighter than Catherine. So, they started lying on her; they would break things and blame it on her. Not do their chores and say that she did nothing. Take things without permission and say that she did it, etc.

This happened often.

Catherine got so many beatings by her mother, that she nearly lost her mind.

Mother would leave bruises on her face, back, arms, and legs. Most of the wounds bled and she never tried to stop the bleeding. Catherine had to take care of it herself.

The other children felt sorry for her sometimes, but those feelings usually passed.

Bernadette used to try and help put bandages on, but Catherine would push her away.

Catherine started to become very bitter towards her siblings.

The older siblings told her that it was better if she got the beatings than them. They knew it was not fair to Catherine. What mother was doing was not fair either.

Catherine tried everything to stay out of trouble, but it was impossible. It was too hard going against all her siblings.

CHAPTER 9

Mother began calling her all kinds of nasty names, like; black heifer, stupid black bitch, ugly nigga, etc...

Mother did not hold back on anything. She hit her with anything she could think of, even if she didn't do anything, mother would beat her just because.

No matter what, Catherine still loved her mother and continued to try to win her affection.

Catherine tried everything to show mother that she didn't have to treat her this way. She did all the chores, trying to show mother that she was a good girl. But it never worked. It was something about her that mother did not like.

A couple of years went by, with the same old, same old going on; Mother continued with her drinking and continued with the beatings.

Mother also continued to have many men over to the house. There seemed to be a party at the house, just about every day.

Mother never got any rest; she just became meaner and meaner.

Chapter 10

One early morning, mother woke Catherine up to go to the store to buy some groceries. She gave her a list a told her not to forget one fucking thing.

Catherine went to the store and got everything that was on the list. The store bagged everything up and gave it to her and she started on her way home.

She was walking, minding her own business while carrying the bag of groceries, and saw a man coming close to her. She pretended that she did not see him but picked up a little speed in her step.

Suddenly, the man approached her.

He said hello and started walking beside her.

He asked her what her name was, but she ignored him and continued to walk at a fast pace.

The man walking next to her, made her feel extremely nervous.

He continued to walk beside her, so she picked up the pace even more.

The man asked her why she was walking so fast, but Catherine said nothing. She just kept the fast pace up.

She didn't know what to do.

She thought to herself, "should I drop this bag and run, no because I will get in trouble with mother. Should I tell this man my name so he would leave me alone).

She decided to keep up the pace and told the man to leave her alone.

The man continued to pursue her. He did not like it when she told him to leave her alone. His voice became deeper and more aggressive.

He said "now, why do you want to act like that. All I was trying to do is be nice to you and you want to tell somebody to leave you alone.

He stepped in front of her, blocking her way "You don't tell me to leave you alone."

He grabbed her and she dropped the bag of groceries. She tried to scream, but he covered her mouth.

She tried to pull away from him, but he was too strong.

He grabbed her tight and pulled her towards a vacant building and into a hallway that had a door.

Catherine continued trying to scream for help.

He whispered in her ear "shut your fucking mouth before I break your neck."

He began pulling and tugging on her clothes and started kissing her and rubbing all over her body with one hand. The other hand continued to cover her mouth.

She kept trying to fight him off by pushing his hands away from her, but her strength could not match his. All she could do was cry.

He held her by her neck with one hand; it was so tight that she could hardly breathe. He pulled her pants down with the other and said "stop all of you whining, you know you want this. You think you can talk to me anyway you want to? Well, I'm about to show you what a real man is. You're about to get all of this dick and you're going to take it."

She tried to scream again, but he was holding her neck too tight. She was kicking her legs, trying to get him off her.

He said in a strong voice "what did I just tell you, you little bitch? Didn't I tell you to stop moving?" He began punching her in her legs, which made her stop moving them.

It seemed like he got stronger with every punch.

Catherine thought to herself, "this was way worse than getting beat by mother.

The man tore her panties off, while one of his hands was still on her neck. All she could do was shake her head, motioning **NO**.

Tears continued to run down her face, but it didn't matter to him.

Then it happened!

CHAPTER 11

He inserted himself into her, shattering her purity and innocence.

He forcefully pushed himself into her vagina and ripped her open completely.

Catherine's eyes opened wide as she held her breath. The pain was indescribable. All kinds of things were rushing through her mind; she just didn't understand what. She didn't know what her body was going through, all she knew was it was more pain than she had ever felt, and she wanted it to stop.

He loosened his grip on her neck, so she began asking him to stop.

He said, "you know you like it, stop acting like you're so innocent" and began thrusting into her harder and harder.

Her voice was so weak because the pain was so severe. She said, "please mister, you're hurting me."

He slapped her across the face a couple of times and said, "Stop whining, you know you like it. Take it you little bitch! Take all of it!"

Catherine began to screech as he plunged further inside her like a mad man. She couldn't help it. It was all her little body could take.

Then he put his hand over her mouth as he continued to ravage her.

He was pushing so hard that the stairs started to push through her back.

She was still screaming, but it was muffled, because he put his hand back over her mouth as he pressed.

Suddenly, she went limp, her violated body could not take anymore.

When he saw this, he thought he had killed her. So, he got off her and ran out the door. He left her there in that vacant hall, nearly naked, bruised, and ravaged.

CHAPTER 12

Catherine awoke sometime later and felt so much pain throughout her body. She looked around the hall for the man, because she was afraid that he was still there. Once she was sure that the man was gone, she began moving slowly trying to get up.

She started crying hysterically while looking for her pants (she didn't want to go home with her private parts all out). She finally found them and put them on slowly. Then she made her way back home.

She walked home slowly because her damaged body would not allow her to travel regularly. Home was a couple of blocks away, but it seemed further than that. People passed her and just looked at her strangely, but no one asked if she was ok.

She didn't care about people seeing her messy or dirty, she just wanted to get home.

She made it home about thirty or forty minutes later.

When She opened the door, she saw no one. She came down the doorway hall, looking for her mom with tears in her eyes. She finally found her mom in the kitchen.

She ran over to her and fell to her knees, all bruised up.

George and Bernadette came from the back to see what was going on.

She began telling mother about the rape when she was interrupted by a question.

Mother asked, "what the hell happened to my damn groceries?"

Catherine was shocked by the question. She looked down and thought to herself, "does she not see the way my clothes are? Does she not see my bruised face? Does she care?

She looked back up and could not take her eyes off mother; she was in disbelief. Her eyes began to dry up as she responded to mother.

She said "mother, I was trying to tell you what happened. I was trying to tell you that I was raped. That is how I lost the bag of groceries."

Tears rolled down her cheeks as she looked for compassion from her mother. She was just looking for a sign that mother cared.

Mother looked down at her with disgust in her eyes and said "How could you let something like that happen? You took your hot ass out there so you could get attention, now look at you. All you were supposed to do was go to the fucking store and bring your fast ass right back home. You couldn't even do that shit right. You make me sick."

Catherine put her face into her hands crying desperately. She said frantically "mother, he hurt me. The man really hurt me. I did what you told me to do. I went to the store and got what you told me to get. He came out of nowhere.

I tried to get away from him, but I couldn't. I didn't say anything. I was walking back home from the store. Mother, he really hurt me. Please mother."

She lifted one of her hands in hopes that mother would grab it and comfort her.

Her mom looked down at her like she was sick to her stomach. Mother said "get your ass up, you act like he killed you. This is just another part of life. Being a female is hazardous to our health. This is something that happens in life, you just have to deal with it. Now go clean your nasty ass up."

She never even touched her.

Chapter 13

George and Bernadette looked at Catherine with sorrowful eyes. They wanted to say something but were too scared of mother to even dare. They were shocked by what they heard.

Bernadette was petrified.

When Catherine started to rise, they turned around and went back into their room. They discussed everything that they heard and made a pact to never lie on her again. The conspiracy against Catherine was no more for them.

She arose from her mother with her head hanging down. Her heart felt so heavy, she put both of her hands on her chest. She thought her heart was about to burst.

She had forgotten about the pain in her body, all she could feel was the pain in her heart. She would have never thought in a million years that her mother had no love for her, until now.

Catherine turned away from her mother and went down the hall to the bathroom. She sat on the side of the tub and started to run her some warm bath water.

What mother said played over and over in her head. Her heart hurt so bad that it was impossible for her to cry. She asked herself; was this what life for girls is really like? Would I have to experience this agony again? Had any of my sisters ever experienced this? Why is this ok with my mother?

The thought of everything just did not make sense. She did not understand any of what was going on. She just felt so unloved.

Once the water for the bath was ready, she began to get herself together so she could bathe.

Bernadette brought her clean clothes to put on. She said "I'm sorry for getting you into so much trouble. I'm also sorry that you hurt. Can I help you with your bath?"

Catherine was deeply moved. It was a relief to know that someone cared. She told her that she could help her bathe. Catherine started crying again; the tears just continued rolling down her cheeks as she was bathing.

Bernadette was shocked to see all the bruises upon her sister's body. She made sure that she rubbed her down gently, so that she would not cause her any pain.

Catherine continued crying while her baby sister washed her down with a cloth. She felt something in her heart change. The love loss from mother made it change.

Bernadette tried wiping the tears with the towel. It really made her feel bad to see Catherine like that. She wished that there was something she could do to make her feel better.

Catherine could not figure out what to do next, she just wanted to put everything behind her. She wished that this day had never happened.

After a few months, everything went back to normal. Catherine did not receive as many beatings, but she still got in trouble.

She and the two youngest siblings began to grow closer.

For the first time, she was not fighting the whole clan.

The rape was never discussed again.

CHAPTER 14

A year or so went by, while mother was still drinking and mingling. There were so many parties, that their apartment became the most popular place in the building.

Mother's drinking was getting worse. Seagram's Gin with grapefruit juice was the targeted pleasure for mother. It became an everyday thing, along with many men coming and going.

She wasn't giving out so many beatings because the children were getting too big. Plus, she had something else in mind.

Although mother loved to entertain, she did not work and was on public assistance. So, her funds were limited. The money she received was not enough to support her drinking habit.

She received money from time to time from the guys she slept with, but it was still not enough. She was getting tired of bedding all the different men. She began wanting someone of her own, so they could take care of her. So, she thought up a new scheme.

Mother decided not to sleep with as many men as she did before because she had her sights set on one. She knew that this guy would not take care of her if she continued to sleep around. Even though he was married, she knew that she had the goods to take him away from his wife. Hell, he was at the house just about every day anyway, so it wouldn't be a hard task to accomplish.

For her to continue drinking, she had to come up with the money. To get the money, she had to give up the goods.

She was tired of the rotation of things, so she decided to go a different route. She decided to give up the dark one.

Mother decided that Catherine should do the deed because she was no longer pure.

CHAPTER 15

Catherine was about twelve years old when her mom told her that she needed to help bring money into the home.

Catherine was stunned by what she was hearing from mother.

She was told that she had to bed some of the men that came to the house to get paid.

Catherine was shocked, she couldn't believe her ears.

Mother said, "don't make this shit into something big, it's not like you are a fucking virgin anymore. You cannot go back and start again, so you might as well use the one damn good talent you have left. You ain't good for nothing else."

Catherine felt such anger and told her mother **NO**. She said, "please don't make me do this."

Mother said in a stern voice "stop whining" and slapped her across the face. You are going to get me some money for my drink. It's not like this shit is something new to you, geeze."

Catherine could not believe that her mother had slapped her. She also couldn't believe the things that were coming out of her mouth.

She began to feel strong anger against her mom. She felt as though she hated her. She couldn't figure out why her mom was doing this to her, it wasn't clear how their relationship got this way.

Mother said "I will beat the hell out of you if you say one more damn thing. We are not going to talk about this any further. When I call you, you'd better come running."

CHAPTER 16

Catherine was angry and conflicted but knew she had no choice. So, she did as she was told.

Mother set up a couple of rendezvous for Catherine.

She had to go to the men's apartment because mother didn't want anyone to know what she had her doing.

When Catherine got the call from mother, it made her angry and extremely nervous. She didn't want to go to anyone's apartment. She didn't know anything about these men, but she knew if she didn't do it, she would get in trouble with mother.

Catherine went to the first guy's apartment on the ninth floor. She stood in front of the door for several minutes before knocking. She was so scared. She didn't know what to expect from this guy.

When the guy opened the door, he greeted Catherine with a Chester cheesy smile.

When she looked up and saw the way the guy was smiling, it made her flesh crawl; this man really creeped her out.

The guy invited her into his apartment. He said while still smiling "hey sweetness, I'm glad you decided to come by. We are going to have some fun today."

She began to walk slowly into the apartment, not taking her eyes off the guy. Her heart was beating so fast that it made the rest of her body shake. She did not know what to expect, nor did she see what was coming.

The guy grabbed her hand and led her to his bedroom. He asked her if she wanted anything to drink. He said "I got some Wild Irish Rose, some Gin, and some Kool-Aid. Which one would you like?"

Catherine said that she did not want anything.

So, the guy says while still smiling "you just want to get down to business, huh?"

She wanted to get up and run, but she knew if she did not come back with the money all hell would break loose with her mom.

She said "my mom said get the money first. So, can we just get that part over with first?"

The guy's facial expression changed. He said, "all I was trying to do is make you a little comfortable, but if this is the way you want it let's get it on."

He placed the money in her hands and began taking his pants off and then his T-shirt. He told her to get in the bed and get up under the covers.

Catherine got under the covers and laid there stiff as a board. She laid there with her eyes closed because she didn't want to see anything that the man was doing.

The guy got into the bed next to her. He asked, "why didn't you take off your clothes?"

She said nothing; she just kept her eyes closed and laid still.

The guy began to rub her chest and stomach. His hands began moving down towards her vagina. He began to pull down her pants and underwear while whispering in her ear "I'm going to make you feel really good. I promise it won't hurt at all, just lay back and enjoy."

Catherine opened her eyes when he began whispering in her ear; it made her feel like she was about to be attacked again. Plus, she didn't know what this man was talking about. She just wished that it would hurry up and end.

The guy started moving her body over from the edge of the bed. He continued rubbing her chest, stomach, and vagina softly while kissing her face and neck.

Her body began to respond to the soft touches. She did not know what was going on with her body, but what he was doing kind of felt good.

The way the guy was touching her made her relax a bit.

The guy saw how Catherine was responding to his touch; this excited him more.

He said, "I am about to get on top of you, so I'm going to need you to spread your legs some so that I can lay in between them."

She began to tense up again.

He said "no, no, don't do that. I'm not going to hurt you, I promise. Just relax and let me in." He opened her legs and began to penetrate her.

Catherine tried to resist the feelings, but she couldn't. She thought to herself, "this feels nothing like the last time.

Her body began to move in ways that she never expected. She ended up matching his movements with hers.

The guy began smiling while looking down at her. He said, "yeah baby girl, just keep going with the flow." Take it all in and enjoy.

Before you knew it, Catherine was totally involved with the situation. She liked the way her body moved and the way the experience made her feel.

The guy took particularly good care of her and was glad she enjoyed the experience. Once they were finished and cleaned up, he told her that he would see her again very soon.

She was surprised that she did not oppose anything that he was saying.

CHAPTER 17

When Catherine came home, she went to mother's bedroom to give her the money.

Mother looked at her and asked with a smirk on her face "did it kill you or did you like all of that dick inside of you?"

Catherine was shocked by what her mother had just said. It shook her to the core.

She was not going to give mother any satisfaction of knowing anything about the experience. She didn't even respond. She just gave her the money and left the room.

Mother said, "I knew you were going to be good for something, SHIIIIT." And, continued counting the money that Catherine gave to her.

Catherine continued to see the guy, along with others. He showed her more and more things about her young body, and he took care of her financially.

She only liked being with him physically and dreaded the other activities with the other men. But she knew she had to do what mother told her to do.

She did this for a year or two, while her mother continued to drink and entertain.

She began to despise her mom, hated her life, and started to hate some of the MEN.

Mother did not have a care in the world, she continued to pursue and persuade the married man stronger than ever.

The married man never had a chance, and he never knew what she had her daughter doing.

The married man ended up leaving his family and moving in. He began taking care of mother, just like she knew he would.

CHAPTER 18

Everyday mother's boyfriend went to work, she invited another man over. He always brought a drink and money. They laughed and drank, enjoying themselves all day. But she made sure that he was gone before her boyfriend got home.

The man would come back over later that evening and hang out with them both.

Mom's boyfriend never had a clue.

Mother loved the way the money was coming in, so she decided to include the other sisters; Tabatha was a couple of years older than Catherine and Bernadette was one year younger.

Mother called the girls into the living room, so that she could give them the news. She told them that she wanted them to do the same thing as Catherine was doing. She told them that it was time for them to pull their weight also.

Mother said, "the house needs money to keep going and you have to go out and make some."

Tabatha was not going for it. She told her mom that she would fight her before she sold her body for her.

She told her mother to go fuck those men herself.

She said, "if I get money for that, I will make sure it goes in my damn pocket first." What kind of fucking mother are you? I wish I would sell my mother fucking body for your sick ass habit! Bitch please!"

Tabatha was one of those girls that you did not mess with. She did not let anyone push her around. If she was forced to do anything, you know that she went down fighting.

Bernadette was a little different. She was truly scared of mother. She tried to do everything she could to stay out of trouble. But with a mother like theirs, it was impossible.

When mother told her that she had to do as Catherine was doing, she took on the task. She did not worry about it at first, because Catherine was going to be with her.

She was kind of excited because they were going to be able to do something together. She had no idea what mother was about to get her into.

Chapter 19

Mother gave them the instructions of whom they would visit next.

Catherine knew the man; she had already been with him before.

Mother told them to let the man choose between them.

This made Catherine truly angry for some reason. She couldn't believe that mother would send baby sister out there to do something like this. She said to herself, "this woman does not have a heart. She doesn't care about anything or anybody.

Catherine decided not to think about it anymore, she just prepared for the task at hand.

When they went to the first man's apartment on the fourth floor, they waited a little bit before knocking on the door.

Catherine asked Bernadette if she was feeling ok. She said, "you know you don't have to do this, don't you?"

Bernadette shook her head motioning no. She said, "I will get in trouble with mother if I don't do what she says."

Catherine said, "we could come up with a plan for you not to do this and mother would never know."

Bernadette thought about it for a minute and said "Naw, we will get in trouble. You already get in enough trouble. I'm not going to help mother do anything else to you."

Catherine looked at her with her eyebrows raised and said, "are you sure you want to go ahead with this?"

Bernadette said, "come on, let's get this stuff over with."

They knocked on the door of the man's apartment. He opened the door with a big smile.

They told him that he had to choose between them.

Since he had already tampered with Catherine, he chose Bernadette.

Bernadette looked at Catherine to see if she had anything to say. All Catherine could do was look at her baby-sister as she walked away with the man.

Bernadette began to fear the man because this was going to be her first time. She didn't know what to expect and she did not know how to respond to the man. She tried to be courageous thinking (if Catherine can do it so can I). But it didn't work.

The man tried to talk sweet to Bernadette.

He said "it's going to be alright. I'm not going to hurt you". He did not know this was her first time and I don't believe he would've cared. He just wanted to get what he could out of her.

He offered her a drink because he wanted her to relax.

Bernadette said, "no thank you."

The man started to get agitated with Bernadette because she would not relax.

She was too tense for him.

All kinds of thoughts started racing through her head. She was really scared. She did not want to go through with the act.

She tensed up more when the man touched her. She pushed his hands away every time he tried to touch her private. She thought of mother and began to let him touch her a little.

When he started trying to lay her down, everything in her became stiff. She jumped up and told him no.

The man was furious! He started calling her out of her name.

He said while holding her arms tightly "you ain't nothing but a tease. Loosen up you little bitch or I'll bash your face in and take it anyway."

Bernadette started yelling for Catherine.

She continued to apologize to the man, but it did not stop him from calling her out of her name.

She said, "I just can't go through with it" and started yelling for Catherine again.

The man continued trying to lay her down.

She said "please let me go.

But he continued to hold tight to her arms.

She yelled again for Catherine while pulling away from the man.

Catherine came barging into the room and told the man to let her sister go.

The man told her to get the hell out of there and mind her business, while still holding Bernadette.

Bernadette was still trying to shake loose from the man.

Catherine told the man again to let go of her sister.

The man said, "if you don't leave right now, I will take both of you."

Bernadette didn't know what to do. All she could do was stare at Catherine. When she saw her facial expression change, she knew something bad was about to happen.

Catherine would not take her eyes off the man holding her sister.

She became so angry that she began to shake. She yelled at the man "TAKE YOUR FUCKING HANDS OFF OF MY SISTER BEFORE I SMASH YOUR HEAD IN."

The man did not see the bat behind Catherine's back. So, he started coming towards her.

Before the man could get all the way up, Catherine charged him with the bat and wacked him across the head.

When the bat made contact, he let Bernadette go. The hit had knocked him out for a moment.

Catherine grabbed her sister, and they began to run. They ran all the way home together without saying a word.

When they got home, Catherine told Bernadette that she would have to lie to their mother.

Bernadette asked, "what about the money?"

Catherine told her that she would give the money to mother.

When she sent them out again, Catherine told her to find somewhere to go and she would come get her when she was done.

Bernadette never went to another man's house again.

Mother continued receiving money from the girls, but she still did not take care of the home like she should have been doing.

The children still went without food sometimes, because her drinking and partying was more important than anything else.

CHAPTER 20

Catherine had no respect for men because she believed they had no respect for her. All they wanted to do was use her body up. They didn't even care how old she was.

Catherine had to grow up fast. She decided to change the way things were going. She wanted to benefit from what she was doing. Plus, on certain occasions, it started to feel good.

She decided that love was for fools, but sex was for benefits and pleasure.

Catherine decided that it was time to get the things that she wanted. After seeing the kind of money that was coming in for mother, she began wanting it for herself.

As she continued sleeping with many men, she felt like she needed something to get her through most of the episodes.

The men had no problem providing her with some courage juice and a little weed.

She started buying clothes that helped make her feel sexier than she already was. She also made sure that she had food to eat, because mother was not keeping up with her end.

She learned how to use what she had to get what she wanted. She did a lot of things that a little girl her age should not have knowledge of. But it got her just about anything that she wanted.

The relationship between Catherine and mother was really bad.

Catherine cursed her mother at any given moment. The words that came out of her mouth were foul.

She would say things like; shut the hell up, suck my bloody puss; even though she never had a period. If you say something else to me, I will cut your fucking throat.

Who would have thought a little girl would have a vocabulary like that.

She cursed mother so bad, that you would have thought she was trying to kill her with her words.

Catherine decided that she would no longer sleep with men for her mother's benefit only; mother would have to get her drinks another way. She felt that she had to take care of herself, by any means necessary.

Catherine decided to drop out of grammar school and started staying out all night. She was drinking and smoking weed. She did just about anything she wanted at the men's expense and didn't have a care in the world.

CHAPTER 21

Catherine and her mom started arguing more and more because she would not give her all the money she had made.

Catherine said "mother, you better get your old as out there and get your own fucking money. You already got that woman's husband living here. You better make sure you're not getting played. As much as you suck on him, your pockets should be full."

Mother looked at her like she could pull her heart out. She said "you little bitch, you better give me my money. I'm the reason why these niggas want your rotten ass. You think they care anything about your black ass. They knew you were easy, and they are just getting what they can. You are nothing but a little whore to them."

Catherine was furious. She wanted to tear mother's head off; in her mind, she saw herself banging her mother's head against the floor repeatedly. She saw her mother's blood running all over the floor.

Catherine said (with a sadistic voice) "you are just jealous that you can't please them like I can. You can't even come close to my talents. Look at you! You're a ran-down old drunk. Your beauty matches the bottle that you drink out of. Look at you! No one will give you any more money, they just want you drunk and laid out so they can fuck you like a raggedy doll. If you think that I am going to give you the money that I worked for, you got to be crazy."

Mother started coming towards her quickly.

Catherine said, "try and take it, you won't reach for nothing else again."

Mother stopped in her tracks. She looked into Catherine's eyes and waved her hands at her. She said, "I'm not scared of you. I'll break your fucking neck."

Catherine said with a strong voice "NO MORE! YOU WILL NOT TOUCH ME ANYMORE."

Mother was shocked by what she said. She stared at Catherine once more. She said "You think you're doing something new? There have been bigger and better than you out there. Trust me, your time is limited also."

Catherine just stood there with her fists balled up. She had nothing else to say.

Mother looked at her angrily and decided to turn and walk away.

CHAPTER 22

Catherine became spiteful and vengeful towards her siblings. She used being dark and beautiful to her advantage.

If her sisters found themselves interested in a boy or young man, she made sure that they saw her.

She did whatever she could to get their attention, and it worked.

She always took the guys from her sisters, only to dump them once she had them.

Bernadette and Tabatha began hiding anyone that they were interested in because they knew they were no match for Catherine.

Catherine started to be the talk of the projects, but that did not stop the boys, young men, and men from coming after her. As long as it benefited her, she did not care about anyone or anything else that was going on.

She talked to men like they were beneath her. She had no love in her heart for them.

She called them all kinds of mother fuckers, lame niggas, and short bastards (pertaining to their penis). She knew how to piss them off and how to reel them back in.

It didn't matter to her, because all she needed them for was money and a few moments in time.

She behaved this way for a little while longer, until she met her match.

CHAPTER 23

About a year went by when a new family moved in next door. This family was a little bigger than Catherine's. They came from Arkansas and talked with a funny accent.

Catherine and her siblings became acquainted with this family rather quickly.

Tabatha liked one of the brothers in the family. Bernadette liked one of the brothers also, but she already had a boyfriend in the neighborhood.

They became good friends with the family.

CHAPTER 24

One day the neighbors had some cousins visiting. These cousins caught the interest of all the sisters; they talked with a much stronger accent. Most were tall and their skin was a bit lighter.

But it was only one that caught Catherine's eye completely.

Catherine went over and introduced herself to the young man by the name of John.

He was very tall, with a muscular build. His skin was the color of a caramel piece of candy. He was very handsome to her.

He was a little older than she was, but not like the other men she played with.

John had a way about himself that attracted women to him.

There were so many girls and women after him in the projects, but Catherine was the one who captured his eye.

He had never seen such beauty in a girl before.

He liked everything he saw; from the way her hair was pinned up, to the way her lips curled when she smiled. The way her neck flowed flawlessly, down to her shoulders, and every curve on her body beautifully matched each other in a complimentary sexy way.

John's eyes were fixed on Catherine, from where she started walking down the porch until she arrived in front of him. He couldn't take his eyes off her; she was simply stunning.

Something about John struck Catherine like never before. It was the way he stood and the way he looked at her that she could not shake.

She said to herself, "what is it about this man that got me feeling so funny? No one had ever made her feel mushy inside. It was like love at first sight, although she didn't know what love was.

She just knew that she wanted to be his.

She said "hello, I'm Catherine.

He said, "I'm John."

They stood there talking like they were the only people on that porch. They could not take their eyes off each other. The attraction was strong and captivating.

They were so focused on each other that they lost track of time. When they finally looked up, it was dark. So, they had to say their goodbyes.

Catherine was already involved with a few other men, but they did not mean anything to her. She was just getting what she could out of them.

Although she could not stop thinking about John, she continued her regular antics with the men. It was just something programmed in her now.

She thought about trying to stop, but she just did not know how. She was not sure if she even wanted to.

She knew that no one would take care of her like she was taking care of herself. She liked eating and buying herself nice clothes from time to time. She also liked the gifts that the guys would give her.

So, why should I stop (she asked herself).

Nothing has happened in her life right now that would convince her to go back to the way things were before.

She was very attracted to John, but he made her feel uncomfortable.

She started thinking of the past and decided to keep her guard up, even though she had made up her mind that she was going to go after him.

CHAPTER 25

John continued to come over, visiting his family and pursuing Catherine. She was just too fine and beautiful not to become his.

John started bringing gifts with him every time he visited. They talked and took walks around the neighborhood.

After a few months had gone by, John decided to ask Catherine if they could start going together; he wanted her bad. He wanted her to belong only to him.

So, he decided to ask her on his next visit.

On John's next visit, he asked Catherine to take a walk with him. He told her that he needed to talk to her about something.

She asked what it was, but he told her to wait until they took their walk.

Catherine was nervous because she could not think of what the conversation could be about. Men always made her nervous. She could never relax around them and was always on guard.

She knew that she was still playing around with other men. She was also sleeping with Bernadette's boyfriend from time to time.

Catherine always liked feeling like she was in control of everything dealing with men. It made her feel powerful and she was not about to give that up.

John planned his approach all that day. He wanted to make sure that he did not scare her off. He did not want to appear anxious, so he played it cool.

There were plenty of girls after him, even Tabatha. But there was something about Catherine that he could not get over. He had not known her long, but his feelings were deep and real. It really caught him off guard.

John wanted things to be perfect so that his question of dating would be well received.

Catherine was puzzled by the request from John. No one ever asked her about too much of anything besides sex, and something about the anticipation of this walk gave her butterflies in her stomach.

She wished the walk would come already so they could get the talk over with.

John went to the store to buy a little teddy bear and flowers. He really wanted to impress Catherine. He wanted to make sure that he covered everything for a relaxing walk and conversation with her.

Finally, the time came for them to meet up and take their walk.

When John came to the door, he had a huge lump in his throat. He was nervous but did not want Catherine to see it. He paused and took a deep breath before knocking. He knocked on the door and waited for an answer.

CHAPTER 26

Catherine heard the knock at the door and paused. She knew who it was but was nervous about it. She had so many things going through her mind. She did not like how John made her feel at all.

She's usually in total control of her emotions.

John knocked again and waited. The door finally opened and there was Bernadette.

She spoke to John and told him that Catherine would be right out.

John waited in front of the door until Catherine arrived.

When he saw her, he lit up. He did not know that just the sight of her would bring him so much joy. He felt goofy but decided to compose himself. He was too cool for this stuff.

He asked Catherine if she was ready.

She came out and closed the door behind her. She said "let's go" with a giant smile on her face.

Before they started their walk, John turned to face her and gave her the little stuffed bear and flowers.

Catherine was stunned. She did not know how to respond, but what she felt was warmth.

She said thank you, but in her mind, she thought (what am I supposed to do with this stuff).

Catherine decided to take the items into the house so that she did not have to carry them.

Catherine told John that no one had ever given her anything like that before. She told him that he was very sweet, and then kissed him on the cheek.

John felt so mushy on the inside from the kiss, but he did not let her now.

They started their walk and John began to talk.

John asked Catherine to be his girl.

He said "I know I have only known you for a short time, but I have strong feelings for you. I don't know why this has happened, but there is something about you that I just can't get past. I don't know what it is, but I know that I want you to be mine and only mine in every way."

All Catherine could do was stare at him. She was caught completely off guard.

John said "I will take care of you if you need me to. I would take you away from here and love you forever. I can make you happy if you let me. So, would you please be my girl?"

Catherine just looked at him for a long time; she was at a loss for words.

She thought to herself while looking at him (what is this man talking about? What is he trying to do to me? Why would he play with me like this?)

Catherine finally spoke saying "I am not sure about anything that you are saying. I need some time to think about all of this. I am not used to this kind of stuff."

John was disappointed by her response. He asked if there was anything he could do to help with her decision.

She told him no, in a strong way. She said "you don't know anything about me. You don't know my life and you don't know me. You can't help me. I can barely help myself."

John said "I did not mean to upset you. I just want to be with you. I just want you to belong to me only. Tell me what to do and I will do it."

Catherine said "there is nothing for you to do right now. I have to try to figure out what this is all about. You will have to give me some time to give you an answer."

So, they walked back to the building and her apartment. John kissed her on the cheek and said sorry again for upsetting you and went on his way.

Catherine was so upset. She did not know how to go about this situation. She thought (What was he trying to do to me? Where was this coming from? Who talks to people like that? What does he want from me)?

Catherine's guards were back up in full effect. She was not going to let him get the best of her. She was not going to let anyone play her like a fool. She knew who she was and what she was. She was used to controlling the situation. She had learned how to do that pretty well. She was not going to let this man sneak in and hurt her.

She knew that she wanted to be with John in a sexual way, she never thought about a relationship. That was the furthest thing from her mind. She was only used to using and being used.

Catherine could not figure out where this guy was coming from. She was thinking (What is he talking about, when he says he wants to take care of me? How does someone like him take care of someone like me? Why would he want to take care of someone like me? Why did he have to mess up everything)?

CHAPTER 27

A few months went by, and John continued to come by every weekend. But Catherine never gave him an answer.

Catherine decided to string the situation along for a while. She did not want to get herself into something she didn't know about. But she decided that she was ready to take what they had to the next level. She was ready to test his parts out.

Even though she was still sleeping with other men; including Bernadette's boyfriend, she decided that on their next meeting, they were going to have sex.

She desired John deeply and she was sure he felt the same.

The weekend was almost here, and Catherine began to plot. It was on a Wednesday when she put her plan together. She was going to sleep with John on Saturday.

She put together what she was going to wear and the style her hair was going to be. She knew how she was going to touch him and the words that she was going to speak.

There would be nothing he could do to resist her. She knew who she was and what she had. No man could turn her down, not even John.

After Catherine's plans were done, she went to Bernadette's boyfriend's house and relieved some tension.

When Saturday arrived, she woke up early that morning to get the ball rolling.

Catherine could not wait for the knock at the door. She could not wait to overtake John with all her planned passion. She could not wait for him to experience what she had to offer.

John did not have a clue what he was about to experience.

This plot had Catherine more excited than she had ever been. There was something about this man that made her feel so different. She just could not put her hands on it. But no matter, she was about to blow John's mind with her performance. This was one thing that she knew she was good at.

Catherine answered the door when John knocked. She greeted him with such a big smile.

This warmed John's heart because, during the previous visits, Catherine remained a little cold towards him.

Catherine smiled at John and gave him a kiss on the cheek. She told him (in a soft voice) that she had a change of plans. They were not going to go on their walk today. She asked him to meet her in the laundry room that was in between his cousin's apartment and hers.

There was so much history in this laundry room. All kinds of stuff happened there because it was so dark. People used it to hang out, get high, have sex, and wash clothes.

There was a light in the area, but people seldom used it. They only used the light to wash their clothes.

Each floor in the building had a laundry facility and most of the time it was used for everything but the laundry.

There was a lock on the laundry door, but it was broken most of the time. If someone tried to get in and the door would not move, you knew someone was in there that did not want to be disturbed. Most of the tenants complained, but the janitors never really did anything about it.

Catherine went back into the house to gather the items that she needed to go into the laundry area. She already did her hair and put on her clothes.

She put a blanket, a candle, matches, a couple of sandwiches, and a jug of kool-aid in a bag and crept out of the house. She did not want anyone to know what she was about to do in the laundry area.

When Catherine came out of the house, she saw John standing by the laundry area door. He had a very puzzled look on his face.

Seeing John's expression made Catherine laugh. She didn't laugh loudly because she did not want anyone to hear her. She kind of ran to the laundry door where John was, pushed him into it, and closed the door quickly.

CHAPTER 28

There were two long wood pieces in the area. She told John to help her place the wood pieces against the doorknob. She wanted to make sure that no one was able to budge the door.

John said, "what's going on Catherine?"

Catherine turned to him and said in her sensual voice "don't you worry about a thing. I am going to take good care of you."

John looked at Catherine with a strange grin on his face. He noticed the outfit she was wearing and "boy" was he pleased.

Catherine took the candle and matches out of the bag. She lit the candle and turned off the regular light by pulling the string. She took the blanket out of the bag next and laid it on the floor. She walked towards John and grabbed his hand.

John just kept smiling.

Catherine whispered, "let me be yours in my way, for right now."

She moved closer to John with his hand still in hers. She held her head back just so she could look up into his eyes. She guided John's hand around her waist towards her butt.

John became aroused easily. He thought that everything about her was just so sexy. So, just one touch from her or even a glaze would have put him in the mood.

Catherine placed her hand around John's neck and pulled him down to her so that she could kiss it. She rubbed her fingers in his hair and caressed his face.

Catherine asked John to lie on the blanket and he did. Catherine asked if he was hungry.

John was not thinking about food currently. So, he told her no.

Catherine sat on the blanket also and began to touch his penis while his clothes were still on. She started rubbing him softly up and down while staring into his eyes.

Her other hand began going up to his chest. There were no buttons on the shirt, so she lifted it over his head.

John had a nice six-pack on his stomach and his chest was very muscular too.

Catherine continued to rub his penis and chest at the same time. She pushed John down on the blanket in a very playful way.

John started to show through his pants.

Catherine climbed on top of John and began kissing him passionately. She felt his desire while on top of him.

John grabbed her butt with a firm grip and began to caress and squeeze.

Catherine became excited from the grip. She had to calm herself down because she was on a mission to concur.

She grabbed John's hands and laid them above his head. She said (in a soft voice) "let me take care of you. Lay back and take it all in."

John was so excited he did not know what to do.

Catherine began to undo his pants.

John had to lift his bottom so that Catherine could remove the pants.

Once the pants were removed Catherine began to touch him all over. She started kissing him on the mouth.

Then she went down to his nipples and began to suck and rub on them one at a time.

John did everything to keep his composure. He continued to try and grab Catherine, but she would not let him.

No one has ever made him feel like this.

Catherine began to go down further while kissing a licking him at the same time. She loved the way his stomach felt. And she loved the way he moved with every touch.

She began to go down further. She placed her hand in John's underwear. She was pleased by what she felt. She looked up at him and smiled and began to pull it out.

John could not believe what was about to happen to him. He wanted her so badly, but he didn't think she felt the same about him. His head was spinning from all the excitement. He could not think about anything else but the way she was making him feel.

Catherine pulled John's penis out from his underwear. She adjusted them so that he would be revealed. It stood straight up as a soldier ready for duty.

Catherine placed her hand around his private and caressed it so gently, touching every special spot. Then she began to kiss and lick every part of it.

John started moaning with pleasure while his body twitched with excitement.

Catherine placed her mouth on him. Her head was bobbing up and down as her mouth had a nice grip. She continued to touch him ever so gently, teasing every nerve. When she feels that he can't take it anymore. She jumps on it.

Although she has had many men, she still feels new.

John can't believe what he's feeling. The inside of Catherine's vagina was hot and tight. He could feel every one of her muscles tightly gripping him. He couldn't believe the control that she had.

Catherine slid down until she consumed every bit of him. She's able to feel him in her stomach.

The feeling is sensational. He is packaged just right for her taste.

John has no other choice but to grab her by the waist, while she's on top of him. He pulls her down just a bit more so that she may feel the intensity. Suddenly, he hears a light screech with a strong moan.

Catherine could not hold her emotions back any longer. The touch of John's hands was so powerful. He gripped every part of her waist and butt.

John pulled himself up a bit while still inside Catherine. He grabbed her shoulders so that he could push her down more. He wanted to fill her every being.

Catherine's head went back while her eyes rolled. The feeling was unreal. She felt herself losing control with every stroke.

John continued to push further and further while holding her tight.

Catherine tried to get up. She wanted to regain control, but he would not let her go.

John flipped her over and lifted her legs onto his shoulders. He placed himself back into her and pushed as hard as he could.

Catherine screeched again while telling him to wait.

John lifted her while her legs were still on his shoulders. John bounced her to and fro, while jabbing her forcefully.

He completely took over. He wanted to show her the man that he was. He wanted her to love everything about him.

Catherine didn't know what to do. The man was truly rocking her world.

John placed her down ever so gently and flipped her over. He placed himself into her again and jammed her from the back.

Catherine was trying to run. She needed to gather herself. This man was knocking her insides apart, but it felt so good.

Every time John pulled back there was relief. But when he returned, it felt like walls were being knocked down. He never let go of her while stroking.

He was creating something new within her.

Catherine had no choice but to give in. She had already had an orgasm several times. After a while, she went limp. She had no more energy.

He had worn her out. But it was not over yet.

When she laid on the blanket and would not get back up when asked, he turned her over and began to kiss her from head to toe.

He started from her mouth and went down to her breast. He massaged them nicely while sucking on her nipples.

He started going down further kissing her tummy and making it down to her vagina.

He opened her legs and began to touch her.

Catherine jumped.

John told her to relax and enjoy.

He touched her some more with his fingers, rubbing her up and down. Then he placed two fingers inside of her while still rubbing.

Catherine's juices were flowing like water. This was so unreal to her, but she could not stop enjoying it.

John stopped rubbing her up and down with his fingers. He left the two fingers in her going in and out and placed his mouth on her.

All Catherine could do was let out a strong sigh "oh my god".

John continued to suck and thrust.

Catherine told him to wait.

But John would not listen. He continued, knowing that she was about to cum.

Catherine felt as though she was losing her breath. She could not take it anymore. She put the blanket over her mouth and screamed with ecstasy.

When John saw her about to cum, he went back inside of her. He banged her repeatedly until they reached their climax together.

When it was over, they both laughed and laughed.

John said "I'll take that sandwich now.

They both ate the sandwiches and drank the kool-aid. Then they got dressed and left the laundry area.

After putting the items away, they went for their walk.

CHAPTER 29

John started coming over during the week. Sometimes he came over and Catherine was not there. He was head over heels for this girl. He thought he had feelings for her before, but now it was something he didn't even plan.

Catherine had feelings for John also, but she continued to live the way she always did. She stopped having intercourse sex with the different men, but she still pleasured them.

She told John that he could not come over so much because she did not want her mother to know about them.

John tried to accommodate her, but it was too hard for him to stay away.

When he came by, he gave Catherine a few dollars here and there. He even bought him a new car and picked her up from time to time.

He took her to visit his mother and father on many occasions. They thought she was a beautiful-looking young lady.

His father really liked the way she looked.

He would always ask for a hug from Catherine when she visited. He would sneak and give her a few dollars and ask her not to tell John.

Once he found out where she lived, he started dropping by; he had certain things on his mind.

Catherine never told John about what his dad was doing. She knew it would be a problem.

John had already told her some things about him that he did not like and did not trust.

John was very protective of her and very jealous. He was on guard with every man that came within arm's reach of her.

It did not matter who it was, because Catherine belonged to him and only him. No one was going to take her from him. He loved her with everything in his body and soul. This was the one that he wanted to marry and was going to make sure nothing got in the way of that: not daddy, brother, sister, or mother.

CHAPTER 30

A month or so went by and Catherine began to feel sick. She did not know what was wrong with her. She kept getting dizzy and throwing up whenever she ate. She could not go out much, because she didn't have the energy. She started sleeping more than usual.

Bernadette was worried about Catherine. She asked what was wrong, but Catherine told her nothing.

Bernadette asked if she could get her anything, but Catherine said no.

Jermaine saw that Catherine was sick also. He asked her what was wrong.

She said nothing to him either.

He became angry with her. He said "I know you heard me ask you a question. What the hell is wrong with you? You around here throwing up and stuff. What you do, go get your nasty as pregnant?"

Catherine said in a smart tone "No! Leave me alone Jermaine. Ain't nobody said or did anything to you. Just leave me alone."

Jermaine said, "you are going to tell me what's wrong with you." He went over to her and grabbed her. He grabbed her by the arms and began to shake her. Then he stopped and pushed her down.

Catherine started crying. She knew she could not win a fight against Jermaine. She was very scared of him. She told him to leave her alone.

She said, "you have no business putting your hands on me."

Jermaine said, "tell me what's wrong with you before I smack the shit out of you."

Catherine screamed, "LEAVE ME ALONE!"

Mother came to the front asking what was going on.

Jermaine said, "I think this little whore went out and got herself pregnant".

Mother smiled and said "NOOOOO, you don't say. Well, who do you think is going to want your spoiled ass now? Let's see you make money now." She laughed and laughed at Catherine. Something about this situation just tickled her to death.

Jermaine got his laugh in also. He truly believed that the system of things was about to change.

Catherine screamed, "I'M NOT PREGNANT!"

Mom said "we will see. You are going to take your nasty ass to the doctor.

Tears started rolling down Catherin's face. She could not believe the things that they were saying to her. She thought to herself", Could it be? Am I really pregnant? Is this really happening? These people are out of their mind.

Tabatha came in and saw all the commotion. She asked what was going on.

Jermaine could not wait to fill her in on things. He burst into laughter and said "this little whore got herself pregnant. Can you believe it?"

Tabatha shook her head while looking down at Catherine. She could not believe her ears. She thought to herself, "could this be true? Is miss everything knocked up? What heads will she turn now?)

Catherine yelled again "I AM NOT PREGNANT. YOU ALL NEED TO SHUT THE FUCK UP!"

Tabatha came out of her deep thoughts and said in a strong voice "You better watch your mouth. You know you better not talk to me like that."

Catherine stopped yelling and looked at Tabatha like she was crazy.

Jermaine and Mom continued laughing.

Catherine wanted to jump up and choke both of them, but she didn't. She said "you don't scare me, Tabatha, I can say what I want. You better not even think about putting your hands on me. As for you two fools, you can kiss my ass." Then she ran out of the house.

CHAPTER 31

Catherine went to a friend's house to use their phone to call John. She let the phone ring about four times, but there was no answer. She was really disappointed because she needed him now. She had too much on her mind and she knew that he could calm her down.

Catherine did not want to go back home, but she wasn't feeling well at all. She did not know what was going on with her. She thought to herself", I can't be pregnant I didn't even get a period yet.

Catherine sat on the porch for a while, hoping that John would come by.

Tabatha came towards Catherine and told her that they would be going to the doctor tomorrow.

Tabatha said "don't make me come looking for you. You make sure you wash your butt and be ready."

Catherine looked at her and turned away. She did not want to go see any doctor. She thought to herself", we never went before, why go now?

The next day Tabatha and Catherine went to the doctor.

CHAPTER 32

Catherine was very agitated because she never liked going to the doctor. She was angry at her big sister for forcing her to go to the doctor. But she was cautious in the way that she spoke to Tabatha because she knew that her big sister had a bad temper.

She was not in the mood to fight today.

Catherine asked "why did you bring me here to see this doctor? I haven't even had my period yet."

Tabatha said "there is something wrong with you and we are going to find out what it is. Your period probably did not get a chance to come because you were sleeping with just about everyone. I'm sure you never paid attention to it anyway."

Catherine said "why wouldn't I pay attention to that? You sound stupid.

Tabatha turned her head quickly and said "I told you last time to watch your mouth. Don't make me slap the shit out of you in this office.

Catherine stared at Tabatha. She wanted to say something else, but she knew better.

Tabatha was upset because she did not want to be there with Catherine. She thought to herself", why am I sitting here? This is not my responsibility. I can't believe this, while mother is lying on her back, I'm her with her child. I'm really getting tired of this.

She looked over at Catherine and said to herself, "I can't stand this girl. Look at her!

She is just a waste of time. How could someone so little be so nasty?

Tabatha had no respect for Catherine. Her dislike for her sister grew more and more each day.

Catherine thought to herself", I need to get out of here. But if I run, she will catch me and beat me down. I don't feel good at all, maybe I should just see this doctor and find out what's wrong with me.

So, they both just sat there not saying anything to one another, and waited for the doctor.

CHAPTER 33

The doctor finally called Catherine's name. She got up and went into the room. She was extremely nervous for some reason. But she did what she was instructed to do anyway.

After the exam, she waited for the doctor to come back in with the results.

She knew she was not pregnant because she never had a period. She could not wait to laugh in her mother's and brother's faces with the news of not being pregnant. She was going to make them feel like shit.

These thoughts made her feel a lot better for some reason. But she still wanted to know why she was not feeling well. So, she continued to wait.

It seemed like she had been waiting forever, but it was only twenty minutes. The doctor came in and spoke with Catherine.

The doctor said "young lady, you have gotten yourself pregnant. That's why you have been feeling ill."

Based on the exam that I performed on you, you should be expecting the child sometime in March."

Catherine was shocked. She asked the doctor "how can I get pregnant without ever having a period?"

The doctor responded, "it may have started, but it never had a chance to complete itself."

Catherine said "I don't understand this. This can't be happening to me. I am too young to have a baby; she was on her way to being fourteen.

The doctor said "you are going to have to start taking care of yourself better. Make sure you make all your doctor appointments." And he walked out of the room.

Catherine sat there stunned. Her mind was racing a mile a minute. She had no idea what she was going to do. She began to cry hysterically. Her whole life had changed in one split second.

When Catherine came out of the room, she saw Tabatha leaving a room also. She wiped the tears from her eyes and said to herself", I wonder what was wrong with her.

Tabatha was surprised to see Catherine come out of her room at the same time she did. The look on her face told it all.

Tabatha asked, "so, what did the doctor say?"

Catherine did not want to tell her, so she acted like she didn't hear Tabatha.

Tabatha asked again "so, what did the doctor say?" She looked sternly at Catherine.

Catherine looked up and squinted her eyes at Tabatha. She knew what that look meant.

Catherine said "the doctor said that I was pregnant" in a smart voice. So, what's wrong with you?

Tabatha asked, "what are you talking about?"

Catherine responded, "I saw you come out of that room."

Tabatha said, "so, that doesn't mean that anything is wrong with me."

Catherine asked, "why would you be coming out of a doctor's room if there is nothing wrong with you?"

Tabatha responded, "you need to focus on your mishap and stop trying to mind my business." You are the one that got yourself pregnant and I am sure you don't know who helped you get that way."

Catherine was pissed now. She couldn't believe what her sister just said to her.

She did everything she could not to curse her out, but she couldn't help it.

She said "who the fuck do you think you are? You don't know nothing about me. How dare you say that to me? You have been sleeping around just as much as I have. If I am a whore, as you say, what does that make you? Your legs have opened and closed just as much as mine have. You just don't get the benefits that I do. While you are out here trying to get someone's attention and love, I am out here getting paid. You will never be able to do what I do or achieve what I have achieved. I'd rather be a whore that gets paid than be one that's broke and alone."

Tabatha came toward Catherine quickly. Her face had turned red from anger. She was about to slap the shit out her but realized that they were still in the doctor's office.

She looked down at her and said "you ain't shit! You think you got it made because everyone chases after you. But tell me this, who is going to chase your pregnant ass now? "

Catherine's head went down for a moment.

Tabatha continued "all your tricks and trades are not going to help you now. While you had everything, so you say, what are you going to have now? Don't nobody want no fat nasty ass pregnant whore. Let's see how the money come rolling in now."

She began to laugh hysterically.

While they were still in the hall of the office, the nurse walked up and told Tabatha to make sure she made her next appointment.

The nurse said, "the doctor wanted to check on you and the baby because your blood level was so low."

Tabatha turned her head quickly looking at Catherine.

All Catherine could do was smile.

Tabatha said "you better not tell anyone. If I hear that you said anything, I am going to kick your ass. And you know I will, you stupid bitch."

Catherine just continued to smile.

CHAPTER 34

Tabatha left out of the office. She did not care how Catherine was going to get back home.

Catherine walked out of the office slowly, with a grin on her face. She felt that some of the weight was lifted off her now. She knew that her sister could not hide her pregnancy for long.

She thought to herself, "I can't wait until they find out, then they will get off me. Everybody thought that I was the only one with hot pants on. I knew that I wasn't the only one doing things, I just knew it. I wonder what they are going to say now.

Catherine made it home finally. Tabatha had not gotten in yet. Mother questioned her as soon as she turned the corner.

Mother asked sarcastically, "so, what did the doctor say? Are you knocked up or what?"

Catherine acted like she did not hear her.

Mother said "I know you heard me you little black bitch! ARE YOU KNOCKED UP OR WHAT?"

Catherine continued to ignore her mother and walked into her room and closed the door. Nothing was going to ruin what she was feeling at that time.

She thought to herself, "I need to call John to let him know about the pregnancy. I will give him a call tomorrow when I get up.

Mother nearly kicked the door off the hinges and said "WHO THE HELL DO YOU THINK YOU ARE WALKING PAST ME LIKE YOU DIDN'T HEAR ME? THIS IS MY FUCKING HOUSE! WHEN I ASK YOU SOMETHING YOU BETTER ANSWER ME!"

Catherine just looked up at her mother and smiled.

Mother became angrier when she saw the smile on Catherine's face.

She said "girl, you better take that grin off your face before I slap you into next week."

Catherine stopped smiling and stood up. She said "I wish you would put your fucking hands on me. I will be the last person that you ever touch."

Catherine had no fear at all of her mother for some reason. I guess the hatred took over everything she felt.

Mother turned red in the face. She could not believe that this little girl just threatened her. She could not believe the audacity.

Catherine started walking towards the door where her mother stood.

She said, "excuse me, I want to leave."

Mother just looked down at her. She did not budge.

Catherine said it again "excuse me, I want to leave."

Mother lunged at her, and she ducked running out of the room.

CHAPTER 35

Catherine continued to run until she was completely out of the house. She ran to the neighbor's house to call John. He did not answer, but his dad did.

She told John's dad what was going on and asked him if he would pick her up and take her to their house.

John's dad said sure (with motives in his voice).

Catherine went back to the house and gathered a few of her things quickly. Then she left as fast as she came and went downstairs to wait for John's dad.

John's dad got to Catherine's house quickly.

Catherine was surprised at how fast he got there. She got in the car, and they pulled off.

Catherine started telling him how upset she was with her family. She told him that she had been trying to get in touch with John but had no success.

She asked, "have you heard from him?"

John's dad told her that he may have been on the road for his job. He said, "that is what most truck drivers did."

Catherine was surprised. She did not know that John was a truck driver.

John's dad continued with "I think he will be back sometime tomorrow. But you can stay at the house for as long as you want.

It looks like you need some much-needed rest."

Catherine smiled and said thank you.

She was glad to have someone in her corner and she did need some sleep.

She could not wait to see John again. She knew that he would be surprised to see her at their house, but she hoped that it was going to be a good one.

CHAPTER 36

Catherine always liked going over to John's house. His family always treated her well. His dad always paid a lot of attention to her, and his mom always had something prepared to eat.

John's mom showed Catherine where she was going to be sleeping. She said, "everything that you need is in this closet. You will have the bed all to yourself. If you need anything else, please let me know sweetie."

Catherine placed her things down and looked around the room in amazement. She never had a room of her own; she had to share with her sisters.

She sat on the bed and started thinking about John; how am I going to tell him about the pregnancy? How will he respond? Will he still want me?

The thoughts just kept running in her head over and over again. The things that Tabatha said continued to play over in her head also.

Catherine thought to herself, "could she be right about the men looking at her differently? I should get as much as I can before I start showing. Should I tell John, or should I wait until I have no choice? WHAT AM I GOING TO DO?

Catherine decided to lie down for a while. She felt really tired for some reason. She had not eaten all day. She was just full of tension and anxiety about being told that she was pregnant.

She had no idea what to do next. She was always good at scheming, but this was something new and quite different. This was about to change her young life forever.

Before she knew it, she had dozed off into a deep sleep.

Catherine woke up a few hours later. She was so hungry. So, she got up and went into the living room where John's mom and dad were.

John's mom asked, "did you sleep well?"

Catherine said "yes! I didn't even know that I went to sleep."

John's dad said, "I bet you didn't. I told you that you looked like you needed some much-needed rest."

Catherine said "well I guess you were right (she laughed a little).

John's mom asked "do you need anything, honey? Are you ready to eat?"

Catherine said "yes, I am truly ready."

John's mom got up to fix her something to eat.

John's dad told Catherine to have a seat in the living room with him.

Catherine's said "no thank you, I am going to go in the kitchen with your wife.

Catherine was so hungry. She did not care about watching TV or chatting with anyone. She just wanted to get something in her system, and she knew that John's mom always had something in the kitchen to eat.

John's mom heated up some smothered pork chops with rice and a biscuit on the side and gave the plate to Catherine.

Catherine began eating the food fast as ever.

John's mom was surprised at how fast Catherine was eating. She just stood there and watched.

Catherine did not pay John's mom any attention. She just kept on eating.

All you could hear from Catherine was moaning and scraping of the plate. The food seemed to have left in seconds before Catherine asked for more.

John's mom asked Catherine if she was alright. She asked, "when was the last time you ate?"

Catherine just smiled.

John's mom continued, "you eat like you're eating for two!"

Catherine's smile disappeared. She said, "why, why would you say that?"

John's mom said, "the only time people eat like that is when they are homeless or pregnant. You are not homeless, but I think you're pregnant."

Catherine looked up at John's mother agitated. She did not want to hear all of this, she just wanted to eat.

John's mom asked, "are you pregnant sweetie?"

Catherine just looked at her.

John's mom said, "its ok if you are, I just want to make sure nothing is wrong with you."

Catherine's head went down.

John's mom said "it's ok honey! You don't have to feel ashamed; it happens to us all.

Catherine looked up at John's mother.

John's mom said, "do you still want some more to eat?"

Catherine said yes.

She wondered why this lady was being so nice to her. This made her feel extremely uncomfortable. She did not know how to talk to John's mother. She was used to all kinds of nonsense when talking to other people in her family.

Catherine needed to find out if this woman was truly this nice or did she have something up her sleeves. Either way, Catherine made sure that her guards were up.

John's mom fixed another plate of food for Catherine and gave it to her.

Catherine ate slowly this time while watching John's mom every move. When Catherine finished, John's mom asked if she wanted some dessert.

Catherine said no thank you, I've had enough.

John's mom said, "if you need anything else, just let me know."

Catherine said "thanks, but I am going to go back in the room and lie down for a while."

CHAPTER 37

She went into the room with all kinds of thoughts running through her head (is she going to tell John before I do? I wonder if she's in there telling John's dad. Should I leave now that she knows? What am I going to do?)

Catherine did not want to go back home yet. She wanted to see John first, but she believed that there is a problem now. She did not feel like going through anything else right now.

She went to sleep again for a few hours. When she awoke John was sitting next to her.

John said "hey there you. What cha doing over here?"

Catherine was all smiles. She said "I have been trying to call you. Everything that could have gone wrong has. I kept getting into it with my family, so I had to get away for a few. I called your dad, looking for you. He told me that you were going to be home soon, so he asked me if I wanted to come over here, so I did."

John said, "wow, that's a mouth full." All he could do is smile.

Catherine said "sorry, I was just letting you know."

John responded, "I got it."

Catherine asked "is it ok that I am here?

John responded, "Yeah! But I do wish you had waited for me. I don't want my father around you at all. So, please do not call him again. Ok?"

Catherine asked, "but why?

John said with a sweet voice, "Catherine, you don't know my father. I don't trust him with anything, especially with you. Please just do like I asked. I will call more now that I know that things are the way that they are with you and your family."

Catherine responded, "Ok! But being here did give me a chance to get some rest. So, I am grateful for that."

John said, "that's fine, but let's keep him out of our business."

Catherine looked at him with a confused expression and nodded her head in agreement.

John said, "thanks".

Catherine said, "John there is something that we need to talk about."

John was shocked and said, "there's more?"

Catherine responded, "Yea, there is a lot more."

John did not like the way that sounded. He looked at Catherine with a puzzled face.

Catherine said, "let me know when you are ready."

John said, "Please let me unwind for a few. I had to drive a long way and I am just getting back. Let me take a shower and get some grub in my stomach and we can talk after that."

Catherine said OK. She was incredibly nervous about the whole thing. She did not know how to start the conversation. She was worried that he was going to dump her. She needed him to be on her side right now. She could not take him rejecting her right now.

Her mind began racing again (maybe I should get out of here before he gets out of the bathroom. I wonder if his mom told him what she thinks. How is he taking it? He is going to be mad at me. I can't take this! I need to get out of here).

Catherine began to gather her things; she was rushing. She wanted to get out of there before John came out of the bathroom. She was walking fast out of the room. She said goodbye to his parents while rushing out of the front door.

When she got outside, she let out a deep breath. She began walking down the street looking for a bus stop. She was not familiar with this neighborhood. All she wanted to do was get as far away from there as possible.

She saw a bus stop sign and started jogging towards it. She did not know that John was right behind her.

John started yelling from down the street, "CATHERINE, CATHERINE, WHERE ARE YOU GOING?"

Catherine did not respond, she just kept on jogging towards the bus stop.

John yelled again while running, "CATHERINE, PLEASE STOP. WHERE ARE YOU GOING?

Catherine yelled while jogging, "STOP FOLLOWING ME, I AM GOING HOME."

John continued yelling and running, "STOP CATHERINE, PLEASE! I WANT TO TALK TO YOU."

He almost caught up with her by now. He started running faster because he did not want her to get away. He finally caught up with her and grabbed her arm. He was trying to catch his breath while trying to talk to her.

After catching his breath, he said "what happened? Why did you leave before we could talk?"

Catherine said, "It's just too much going on. I can't deal with anything else."

John asked, "what did I do or not do? Give me a chance to make it up. Please, don't leave, I want you to stay. I love you, Catherine."

Catherine stopped pulling away. She was shocked by what John said. Not one word would come out of her mouth, all she could do was look at him with sad eyes.

This man knew nothing about her, but he just told her that he loved her. She did not know what to do. It felt good hearing it for some reason. It also scared the daylight out of her. No one has ever said that to her before.

John asked, "did you hear me? Please don't go. I want you to stay with me."

Catherine began to cry. She said, "don't do this to me. Don't play with me right now. I can't handle all this stuff. Please, you don't understand. Please, don't do this to me."

John was confused. He did not know what he had done wrong. He could not follow her train of thought. He needed to know where she was coming from.

Catherine said while still crying, "you don't know me. You don't know my life."

John responded, "then let me in. Tell me what's going on with you. Let me help you, Catherine."

Catherine paused for a minute. She had all kinds of thoughts running through her head. She did not know where to begin.

John continued, "you can trust me. All I want to do is take care of you, please let me." He grabbed her again and hugged her.

Catherine was very tense at first, but then she started to relax. She felt such comfort in John's arms.

They began to walk back to John's house. John was still holding her close while walking.

CHAPTER 38

When they arrived back at the house, John's mom asked if everything was alright.

John just held up one finger and continued to walk towards the bedroom with Catherine.

John grabbed the bags from Catherine and placed them in the closet. He sat her down on the bed and continued to hold her. He said, "everything is going to be alright, I promise" in the most compassionate voice.

Catherine said, "no it's not" in such a soft voice.

John said "we are going to wait until tomorrow to talk. You and I need to get some rest. Everything can wait until tomorrow, Ok!"

Catherine and John laid down on the bed.

John began to caress Catherine's back.

Catherine began to feel better. The tension was easing right out of her.

John began kissing her and rubbing every part of her body.

Catherine became aroused.

John whispered, "I love you" in Catherine's ear.

Catherine started pushing him away.

John said softly, "no, don't push me away. Let me love you, Catherine. All I want to do is love you." He continued kissing and rubbing on her.

Catherine's emotions were in overdrive.

She could not resist the feelings of John's touch and she loved the way his lips felt on her skin. She eventually stopped pushing him away and gave in.

John began to undress her. He sat up and took off her shoes and socks. He made his way up to her pants button and began to unbutton them. He pulled them all the way down to her feet and then yanked them off.

He made his way back up by licking her from her toes up to her inner thighs.

Catherine could not believe the feelings that were coming up in her. She didn't know what was going on with her body.

John continued kissing her body while lifting her shirt. He kissed everything on her upper body. He pulled the shirt off over her head and began to kiss her lips ever so gently.

Catherine did not understand what she was feeling. She felt like she was melting on the inside and all of it was coming from in between her legs.

John's hand moved back down her body towards the wetness. He placed his hands in her panties and began to pull them off; they were a little soaked.

John lifted Catherine off the bed and carried her into the bathroom. He put her down and turned on the shower.

All Catherine could do was stare at him. She thought to herself, "what is this man trying to do to me?

John told her to get in the shower. When she did as he asked, he followed her.

He took a towel and soap and began to bathe her. He washed her ever so gently from her head down to her feet. He massaged her back as the water hit her and then he went down to her knees.

Catherine felt like she was on cloud nine.

John looked up at her as the water was running. He grabbed her breasts and caressed them with a nice firm grip. One of his hands began to scroll down towards her belly, while the other stayed on her breast. The other hand followed as he kissed her belly and moved further down.

Catherine could not feel her juices flowing, because the water from the shower was all over her.

John began to kiss her most precious part. He spread her legs open softly.

The warm water touched the inside of her precious part. This gave Catherine a wonderful sensation.

John placed his mouth on her precious part and began to suck and kiss.

John's hands began to climb again towards Catherine's breast.

Catherine's eyes began to roll. Her legs were wide open for anything that he had to offer.

John's hands came back down and grabbed her butt. He pulled Catherine closer to his mouth as he latched on with a nice suction.

Catherine began to moan loudly. She was on the verge of climaxing.

John stopped suddenly; he told her to wait a minute.

Catherine was a bit frustrated that he stopped. She wanted him to continue because she was at her peak.

He got up from his knees and left the shower and came back with a huge dry towel. He told Catherine to step out of the shower.

Catherine hesitated but did as he asked.

John wrapped Catherine in the towel and picked her up and carried her back to the bed; he was still naked.

He laid her down ever so gently and removed the towel. He started rubbing her down with baby oil.

Catherine became more relaxed than she ever had been in her young life. She just accepted everything that was being offered to her by John.

John continued to rub her down and massage her from her head down to her feet. By the time he was done, Catherine was fast asleep.

John stopped massaging Catherine and placed a blanket on top of her. He then climbed over her and laid beside her. He placed her in his arms and fell asleep also.

CHAPTER 39

Catherine awoke the next morning in John's arms. She really liked the way it felt. A big grin came upon her face as she turned to look at him. She said to herself, "I think I could get used to this. This man has won me over.

Catherine began to sit up.

This woke John up. He said, "good morning."

Catherine responded, "morning."

John asked, "how are you feeling this morning?"

Catherine responded, "I'm fine."

John asked, "are you hungry?"

Catherine responded, "for some reason, I am starving."

John got up and went into the kitchen to fix them something to eat.

John's mom heard all the noise in the kitchen and got up to see what was going on. When she arrived, she saw him going through her cabinets. She said "boy, what are you doing in my kitchen?"

John responded, "I am about to fix me and Catherine something to eat."

John's mom responded, "let me do that for you all. You should use this time to talk to Catherine. I believe there is a lot that you both need to talk about."

John looked surprised. He said, "What do you mean?"

John's mom said, "I don't mean anything. Just let me cook this breakfast for you all, so you can spend some more time together."

John walked out of the kitchen looking back at his mom.

John's mom just smiled and began to cook. She waved her hand at John telling him to go on.

John went back into the room where Catherine was. He had a puzzled look on his face.

Catherine asked, "what's wrong?"

John said, "nothing, my mom just said something strange to me."

Catherine asked, "what did she say?"

John responded, "she said that we need to spend some more time together so that we could talk. I wonder what she means."

Catherine lost all the color in her face after hearing what John said.

John asked, "is there anything specific that we need to talk about?"

Catherine looked up at him nervously.

John asked, "what's wrong Catherine; with a concerned look on his face?"

Catherine asked him to sit down. She said, "there is something that I need to talk to you about."

John responded, "what is it?"

Catherine paused for a minute.

John said, "come on Catherine, you can talk to me about anything."

Catherine just looked at him. She had all kinds of thoughts running through her mind. She was so nervous, she wanted to run out of the room.

John grabbed Catherine's hand and looked at her with such kind eyes.

This eased some of the tension in Catherine.

Catherine began to speak, but before any words came out, she jumped up and ran to the bathroom. She started throwing up aggressively.

John jumped up to see about her. He asked with a concerned voice, "are you alright?"

Catherine continued throwing up.

John got a towel and wet it. He gave it to Catherine.

After a few minutes, Catherine stopped throwing up and grabbed the towel.

John did not know what to do. He asked, "do you need me to get anything for you?"

Catherine said no, while wiping her mouth with the towel.

She came back into the room and sat down. She began to cry and talk at the same time.

John said, "hold on a minute girl (with a smile on his face), Calm down first and then we can talk. I can't understand anything you are saying."

Catherine took some deep breaths while wiping her face.

He reached over and grabbed her and wrapped his arms around her. He said, "you don't have to worry about anything I will be here for you."

She said, "no you won't. This situation is going to change everything."

John was shocked at what she said.

She continued "John, I'm pregnant! I know you don't want anything else to do with me, so I'm about to leave.

He sat there on the bed stunned.

She picked up her bags and began to leave the room.

He said, "hold on a minute girl. What did you just say?"

Catherine turned and said with a smart tone in her voice "I'm pregnant! Do you hear me now?"

John could not believe what he was hearing.

She left the bedroom and headed towards the front door. She grabbed the handle of the door and twisted it.

He ran up and grabbed her. He picked her up and carried her back to the bedroom.

She said in a loud voice "put me down, I'm going home."

He said "stop acting like a little kid. Now, sit your but down and let's talk about this."

She said "there is nothing to talk about. I know things are different now. I know you don't want anything else to do with me."

He said, "can you stop talking and thinking for me."

She stopped talking for a moment.

He continued "Catherine whether you believe me or not, this is a good thing. Now I can show you how much I care and want to take care of you. I love you girl! Why can't you hear me when I tell you that?"

Catherine began to cry again. She was an emotional wreck.

He said "let me take care of you and the baby. Let me love you."

She said, "men always say things to get what they want and when they get it, they have no more use for you."

He said "I am not those guys, let me prove it to you.

She responded, "I don't know how."

He said "you don't have to worry about nothing. Just let me show you what I am about and what I can do for you."

Catherine wiped the tears from her eyes and looked at him very strangely. She did not know what to make of this guy. She said "you don't know me, John. You don't know anything about me and if you did you would not like it."

He responded "what you did in your past is your business. It's time for us to build a future with each other. I will get you a house to live in, I will make sure you have nothing to worry about and I will take care of both of you as long as you are mine."

Catherine could not believe the things she was hearing. She thought to herself, "how can someone care for a person like this. He doesn't know anything about me but wants me to trust him with my livelihood. How am I supposed to let this man into my heart, when all I have is pain there? How do I accept what he's offering?

He asked "will you give me a chance? Will you give yourself a chance?"

She told him that she would have to think about it. She asked if he would take her home. She had had enough for one day.

He asked her to stay for a few more days.

She responded, "I just wanted to go home. I need time for all of what you said to sink in. I didn't see this conversation going this way and I did not expect you to say the things that you did."

He didn't know what else to say, so he told her that he would take her home.

When Catherin was getting out the car, John told her to call him when she needed him. He told her that he was getting things in order so that she would see what he was talking about. He slipped her some money and told her that he would see her soon.

She was a little surprised when he gave her the money. She took it, smiled, and walked away.

When she turned and looked at the building, a strong sense of grief came upon her. She didn't want to go back to the house, but she had nowhere else to go.

Catherine said to herself, "back to home sweet home" with a frown on her face.

CHAPTER 40

Catherine entered the doorway of her apartment. As soon as she turned the knob, there was Jermaine. All she could do is drop her head and let out a soft groan.

He said, "well, well, the little slut has returned. How much money did you make out there fucking around this time?"

Catherine just looked at him. She was on guard because she never knew what was going to happen next with Jermaine.

He continued, "What's wrong little slut? No one wants to pay a pregnant whore to play with their dick.

Catherine began walking towards their room. She was not trying to get into it with him today.

Mother came out of her room and met her in the hallway. She asked, "where the fuck have you been you little bitch? Did you get my money?

Catherine looked up at her mother with fire in her eyes and said, "I told your stupid ass that I was not giving you any more money."

Mother called Jermaine. She said, "did you hear this little bitch? She stays gone for days and she thinks she could come back in here with no money. Did you hear what she called me? I should bash her head in right now."

Catherine was scared now because Jermaine was behind her, and mom was in front. She knew if they started fighting, she would not win, but she was surely going to give it a shot.

Mother moved closer to her, she pulled her hand back and brought it forward as hard as she could.

She slapped Catherine so hard that she spent in a circle grabbing the wall so that she would not fall to the ground.

Catherine gained her balance and lunged at her mother.

Jermaine grabbed her from the back and slung her into the living room. He jumped on top of her and began punching her in the chest and arms.

Catherine's baby sister and brother heard the commotion and came running out of the room. They were screaming at Jermaine to get off her.

Mom ran over and began to check her pocket while Jermaine was still on top of her. She took all the money that Catherine had, then told Jermaine to get off her.

Jermaine responded in an aggressive tone "you don't tell me what the fuck to do, this little bitch had it coming."

Mother shouted "GET THE FUCK OFF HER, I SAID. I GOT WHAT I WANTED."

He responded, "I don't give a fuck what you got, don't tell me what to do. I should've let her whoop your drunk ass."

Mother was shocked by what Jermaine had said.

Catherine was screaming for Jermaine to get off her.

He slapped her across the mouth and told her to shut the hell up.

Bernadette and George began to cry while pleading for Jermaine to get off Catherine.

Jermaine told them both to get their little asses back into their room.

He turned back to Catherine and said, "you have no idea how much I hate your fucking guts, do you? You think you can just do whatever you want around here. I bet you if I pressed my knee in your stomach, I could kill that little bastard of yours."

Catherine began to cry and wiggle even more. She did everything she could to get out from under Jermaine, but it was no use.

He began to press his knee into her stomach. This made her throw up, she was on her back, so she started choking on her vomit.

Jermaine began to laugh and before you knew it mother cracked him across the head with a broomstick; he fell over quickly.

Catherine rolled over continuing to throw up. She was coughing and gagging at the same time while tears were rolling down her face.

Mother said, "I told your dumb ass to get off her. I told you I had what I wanted. Shit! It looked like you were trying to kill the girl."

Jermaine held his head while looking up at his mother. He started to say something when she whacked him again.

Mother said, "I'm not scared of you boy, you're fucking with the wrong one. You have no idea what I would do to you. If you want to see, just try me. Go ahead, try me, please.

Jermaine got up holding his head, he was furious. While he was about to walk away, he kicked Catherine in her hip. He said, "that little bitch don't need no kids anyway." He went into the bathroom to check on his head and then left the house.

Catherine was still throwing up. She grabbed the side of her hip and began to get up.

CHAPTER 41

Mother said with a humorous voice, "I bet you'll think twice before you mouth off again, huh? Clean that shit up before you go in that room. You need to be on your knees thanking me for saving your lousy ass life. Shit! That boy was about to take you out of here.

Catherine was sick and pissed off at the same time. She was bending over holding her side while cleaning up her mess. She wished that she were big and tall enough to stand toe to toe with them both.

Tabatha came in while Catherine was cleaning up. She asked, "what the hell happened here?

Catherine said nothing, she just kept cleaning up.

Mother came out of her room and went to the living room. She saw Tabetha and said, "hey girl, where you been?

Tabatha got an instant attitude. She said "what you want to know for? Don't be asking me no questions like that. Why don't you try telling me what the hell happened here."

Mother said with a smirking voice "your sister didn't want to give me what I asked for, so things got out of hand. Hell, your brother tried to kill the damn girl. Can you believe that?"

Even though she and Catherine did not get along much, this news pissed her off.

Tabatha said in an angry voice "how the fuck did you let that happen? What kind of sick bastard are you? You are supposed to be our mother. Man, you are so lucky. The way that I feel right now, ooh. I could just choke the shit out of you right now. You are worthless and I wish I was never born into this sick ass family."

Tabatha looked at Catherine with sad eyes, but she could not bring herself to say anything to her. She turned and stormed back out of the door.

Mother looked dumbfounded. She could not understand why Tabatha was so angry. She said "oh, well" and went back into her room.

Catherine continued to clean up her mess and then herself.

Bernadette and George came to the bathroom to check on her.

Catherine told them to leave her alone. She said "I don't want to talk with anyone right now. Please, just leave me alone."

They left and went back into their room.

After Catherine cleaned herself up, she went into the room to lie down. What happened played repeatedly in her mind. The resentment built more and more in her heart. She couldn't believe this stuff just happened to her. Getting robbed by her mother and almost killed by her brother, who would've thought.

After laying there for a while, she eventually went to sleep.

When she awoke, she felt such pain in her body; everything hurt.

Bernadette was sitting on the edge of the bed. She asked "are you ok? Do you need me to get you anything?

Catherine said with a smart tone, "do it look like I am ok? Man, what do you want? Get away from me."

This made Bernadette very sad because all she wanted to do was help her.

Catherine continued, "get away from me. I don't need anything from anybody!"

Bernadette just went into the room with George. She told him that Catherine was in a bad mood and to stay away from her for a while.

Catherine had to plan out her next move. She didn't want to continue going through things like this with her family. She started thinking of the offer that John made her. She also thought about the money that her mother took and knew that she had to get some more money in her pocket.

She planned her strategy of getting some funds in her pocket and she knew just who to call.

CHAPTER 42

Tabatha came back into the house, still mad about what she heard. She looked around the house for a moment and did not see anyone. She started walking down the hallway towards her mother's room.

She heard noises coming from the other side of the mother's bedroom door; she was entertaining a guest. She placed her ear to the door to see if she could recognize the voice. She did and it was the voice of the neighbor from down the hall.

She thought to herself, "what is he doing here, he is married. Boy, it takes all kinds.

She knocked on the door. She heard a lot of commotion on the other side. So, she knocked again.

Mother said, "who the hell is it?"

Tabatha said, "open the door mother I need to talk to you."

Mother opened the door with a strong pull. She said "what the hell do you want? I told you not to knock on my door when I have company."

Tabatha said, "I need to talk to your dumb ass."

Mother responded, "there is nothing in the world that important, especially coming from you."

A frown came upon Tabatha's face. She said "you are just a lousy, good for nothing, old bag. I hate that I'm even connected to you." She turned away from her and began to cry.

Mother was shocked but a bit amused to see her crying. She could not believe her eyes. She could not believe Tabatha was crying.

She said, "what the hell is going on with you? What are you crying for?"

Tabatha did not know what was going on with her. She wiped her face quickly. She had to get control of herself. She was not going to give her mother the satisfaction of seeing her shed a tear.

When she heard the tone in her mother's voice, she became angry, and all the tears dried up.

Tabatha said, "oh, so you think it's funny. I guess you think that I am a joke. Boy oh boy, if you were not my mother, I would slap that smirk right off your fucking face."

Mother was shocked and the smirk left her face. She looked at Tabatha like she was crazy.

Tabatha continued "you up in here with this married man. I hope his wife catches you and bust both of your heads. It's sad that you are going to be a whore for the rest of your life, that's why your daughter is like she is. Ugh, you are just a waste of my time."

Tabatha walked away and went into the bedroom.

CHAPTER 43

Tabatha had to figure out what was going on with her. She was not one of those girls that went around crying about everything. She was the most dominant girl in the house. She did not take anything off anyone. She was always ready to fight in a split second.

So, what in the world was going on with this so-called strong girl?

She lay down on the bed for a while.

Catherine was in the room also, but she did not bother her.

Tabatha had all kinds of thoughts going through her head. She did not understand what was going on with her body, nor her mind. All she knew was that she had to get a handle on it.

She couldn't let people see her crying and feeling sad about anything. No one in that house had sympathy for anyone. So, she was not about to let anyone get the upper hand on her.

Tabatha turned in the bed towards Catherine. She wanted to ask if she was alright, but she would not let herself do it.

She looked at Catherine and Catherine looked back at her. There were no words exchanged. After a few moments, Tabatha just turned back over and fell asleep.

Catherine just changed views and continued to focus on what she had to do to put money back into her pocket.

CHAPTER 44

Catherine had a couple of men that she knew would give up the money quickly. She had to decide between her first customer and her sister's boyfriend.

Both had strong attachments to her and would go out of their way for her.

She had to make sure that she played it the right way so that neither one would become wise to what she was trying to accomplish.

In truth, she didn't want to be bothered by either one, but she had to do something to get some money back into her pocket. She knew that mother wasn't going to use the money for food or anything for the house, so she had to make sure she took care of herself.

She went to her sister's boyfriend's house to see if he was there. She knocked on the door a couple of times and waited for a response. But there was nothing.

She knocked on the door a couple more times, but still, there was no answer. So, she left going back to the building.

Catherine got back to the building and went upstairs. She knocked twice and the door opened.

The guy opened the door, and a big smile came on his face. He was happy seeing her at the door.

He told her to come in and opened the door wider.

Catherine smiled a little bit and started walking through the doorway.

He said with a chipper voice "it is good to see you, what brought this surprise on. I didn't expect you to come by again until sometime next week.

She said "I was just thinking about you. Is it ok that I came by?

He responded "sure, sure, no problem at all. It's always good seeing you.

She smiled a bit.

He said "come on, have a seat. Is there anything I could get for you?

She said in a coy voice "no thank you, I'm fine.

They chatted for a little while before he began touching her. He was easily excited when she came around.

Catherine decided to play it off for a minute.

She said "boy, you better keep your hands to yourself. Don't start nothing you can't finish, now.

He responded "CAN'T FINISH! Who you talking about can't finish? Hell, I taught you the ropes."

She said with a smirk on her face, "yeah, yeah, so you say."

He looked at her like she was crazy and said, "girl, whatchu talking about. You know ain't no lame in my game. Wait a minute, enough of all this talking, let's go.

She looked and said, "where we going?

He stood up and bent over, picking her up. He carried her to the bedroom. He laid her down so gently and began kissing her.

She said "hold on, this is not what I came here for.

He responded "maybe not, but here we are. Are you going to deny me or what?

She just looked at him with puppy eyes.

He said "so, what is it going to be? Me and you right now or what?"

She grabbed him by the neck and began kissing him. She knew most of his spots because he showed her.

She grabbed his shirt and began pulling it over his head and then began unbuttoning his pants.

He became so excited. He grabbed her shirt and began unbuttoning it slowly.

She continued kissing and licking his body. This made him move a little faster with the removal of the clothes.

She said with a smirk 'don't rush, I'm not going anywhere.

He stopped her from kissing him and laid her down on the bed. He rubbed her face and said 'thanks for coming by it was a great surprise.

CHAPTER 46

About six months passed, Catherine and Tabatha began to show. Tabatha hid her pregnancy better than Catherine did.

Tabatha made sure that she did not eat a lot and made sure the clothes she wore were a little too big for her. She made sure that she stayed away from everyone as much as she could. She was not going to tell anyone until she was ready.

She saw how Catherine was treated when they found out and she was not going to give them the chance to do that to her.

Catherine continued to grow. She ate what she wanted and dressed how she wanted.

John took good care of her by making sure she always had money in her pocket; he did not know that she was getting her own money her way.

Even though Catherine was pregnant, she continued sleeping with other men to get money. It wasn't as many as before, but she still had her picks.

She was one of the best-dressed pregnant girls in the projects. It was hard for those men to stay away from her even though she was pregnant.

She kept herself groomed and fed. She did not want for anything.

CHAPTER 47

John was still trying to prove himself to Catherine.

Whenever he was in town, he made sure he came over to see her. He made sure she had everything that she wanted and made sure that she only spent the night at his house when he was in town. He did not want her to be there when he was not there.

Catherine felt like she was on top of the world. Everything that she thought was going to happen didn't and the men still wanted her company. She was so happy to know that her family was wrong.

Catherine and Jermaine still argued, but he did not put his hands on her while she was pregnant. He continued to put her down as much as he could, but she didn't pay him no mind.

Catherine wanted to talk to Tabatha about the baby that she was about to have. She just did not know how to approach her.

Tabatha was tuff and at any moment she would start swinging. Her emotions were all over the place these days.

Catherine knew she had to play it safe while talking with Tabatha about her pregnancy.

CHAPTER 48

One day, Catherine was standing on their cold porch minding her business and one of her associates came up to her. He asked if she had heard the rumors going around about her brother Jermaine.

Catherine did not know what he was talking about, because she had heard nothing. She asked, "what the hell are you talking about?"

The guy said, "there is a rumor going around the building about your brother."

Catherine responded, "so, what's the rumor?"

The guy said, "are you sure you haven't heard anything?"

Catherine responded, "I just told you that. Stop going on with this bull, just tell me what it is that you've heard."

The guy told Catherine that a rumor was going around that her brother Jermaine was seen coming out of another man's house.

Catherine said, "so! What's that supposed to mean?"

He said, "they saw Jermaine coming out of the house zipping up his pants. The guy that live there is known for messing with boys in the building."

Catherine said, "STOP! My brother may be a lot of things, but he is not a fag."

The guy said, "I did not say that he was a fag. I'm just telling you what's been talked about around the building. Don't get mad at me!"

Catherine asked, "did you see him coming out of the apartment?"

The guy said, "no."

Catherine continued, "well, be careful of what you share with people. You know Jermaine, if he heard you say something like that, he would snap out. He would come after anyone and bash their heads in.

All I am saying is, you better be careful who you share this stuff with."

The guy said, "listen out for what's being said and then you will see what I am talking about. I would never say that about him, but this is what's going around the building. I just thought I should tell you."

Catherine said thanks and turned away from the guy and walked back to the apartment.

CHAPTER 49

When Catherine came into the house, she heard arguing. It was Tabatha and mom.

Mom had busted in on Tabatha in the bathroom and found out that Tabatha was pregnant.

Tabatha was yelling, "GET OUT OF HERE YOU STUPID BITCH. YOU AIN'T GOT NO RIGHT TO BUST IN ON ME LIKE THIS."

She was trying to cover herself while yelling.

Mom started laughing. She said, "so, that's why you been sleeping all day and been moody as hell. I knew something was going on."

Tabatha continued yelling, "YOU DON'T KNOW NOTHING, YOU NOSEY BITCH. YOU NEED TO BE MINDING YOUR OWN BUSINESS. YOU ALWAYS TRYING TO FIND OUT SOMETHING."

Mom continued to look at her and laugh.

Tabatha said with a stern look on her face, "I don't see nothing funny. You are so fucking retarded. I can't stand your stupid ass. I hate your fucking guts.

Tabatha was furious and began acting like a savage beast lunging at her mom.

Mom jumped; she was surprised at Tabatha's reaction. She screamed, "CALM DOWN CHILD. WHAT THE HELL IS WRONG WITH YOU?"

Tabatha continued towards her mom. She ended up knocking her down on the floor next to the bathroom and landing on top of her.

Tabatha yelled, "I TOLD YOU NOT TO MESS WITH ME!" She grabbed her mom by the neck and began to squeeze."

Mom was gasping for air while trying to fight Tabatha off.

The children ran out of the room. They screamed, "TABATHA, WHAT ARE YOU DOING?" They ran over towards mother and her. They tried everything to pull Tabatha off, but she was just too strong.

The children continued while crying and pulling on Tabatha "LET GO, LET GO, IT'S YOUR MOTHER TABATHA. PLEASE, LET GO!

She paid them no mind. She was in another world of her own, while choking her mom.

The rage had taken over.

Catherine came running down the hall. She said in a panicked voice, "girl, what the hell are you doing? Get off her!" She put her arm around Tabatha's neck. She grabbed her hand with the other and began to pull backward.

Tabatha let her mom go. She fell back on Catherine.

While pulling Tabatha back, Catherine fell to the floor hard. She got the wind knocked out of her.

Tabatha turned over and began punching Catherine.

Catherine was blocking as much as she could.

Catherine was yelling while trying to protect herself from Tabatha, "GET OFF OF ME YOU CRAZY ASS FOOL. WHAT THE HELL IS WRONG WITH YOU?"

Tabatha was acting like she had lost her mind. She went completely off. She kept swinging on Catherine with full force.

No one could calm her down.

The next thing you know, mother knocked her across the head with the broom stick.

Tabatha screamed so loud that it shook everyone's core. No one knew what to do with her.

She grabbed her head, turned, and looked at her mother and ran at her again.

Jermaine came in and heard all the commotion. He looked down the hall and saw everyone.

He saw Tabatha running towards mother.

He ran down the hall and grabbed her.

He said while holding Tabatha's hands, "what the hell is going on? What is wrong with you girl?"

Tabatha said nothing, she just continued trying to get to mother. The look in her eyes was deadly. She looked like she wanted to kill her.

Jermaine continued holding Tabatha. He asked mother what was wrong with the girl.

Mother said, "this crazy ass heifer then got herself pregnant, and she mad because I found out."

Tabatha said with a strong voice "you need to mind your own fucking business. I am tired of you." She lunged at mother again.

Jermaine was shocked, but he continued to hold Tabatha. He told her to calm down.

Tabatha shouted, "LET ME GO JERMAINE!"

Jermaine paid her no attention. He said, "you better calm down before you make me hurt you. Now, I'm trying to be nice, but don't push it. If you put your hands on mother again, I am going to have to put you down."

Tabatha stopped trying to pull away. She turned towards Jermaine with an evil look on her face and told him to let her go.

Jermaine started smiling. He said, "don't make me show you how crazy we both are."

He let her arms go and stood on guard.

Tabatha rubbed her wrists and jumped at Jermaine.

Jermaine was a little shocked by the move, but he ended up slamming Tabatha to the floor.

He knocked all the wind out of her.

Jermaine was very strong, but Tabatha did not care.

Tabatha continued trying to fight Jermaine while on her back.

Jermaine slapped her a couple of times while trying to talk to her. He could not get through to her, so he told mother to call the police.

CHAPTER 50

Mother ran to the neighbor's house and asked if they could call the police for them.

The police arrived and saw that Jermaine was still holding Tabatha down. They ran over and pulled him off her and put him against the wall and began to handcuff him.

Mother said, "stop you fools, he was holding that crazy ass fool down, because she kept trying to attack me."

Tabatha got off the ground and lunged at her mother again.

Catherine grabbed her again.

The police saw what Tabatha was doing and they let Jermaine go and went after her.

Tabatha began fighting the police. They put her hands behind her back and pulled them up to stop her from acting up.

Mother screamed at the police "BE CAREFUL, SHE'S PREGNANT!"

One of the policemen said "you should have told us that in the beginning mam. This information presents a new view of things. The way that she's acting means that she needs to be committed. She seems to be a danger to herself and others. Would you like us to take her to the hospital?"

Mother said yes. She said "somebody needs to give her some medication. This girl is out of her mind."

The police took Tabatha out of the house.

She was still pissed. If looks could kill, everyone would have been dead on that day.

The police got Tabetha down stares placed her in the police car. They told mother that they were going to take her to the mental hospital.

The policeman said, "we really think she needs some help with her mind. We can't leave her here because she has presented herself as a threat to others and herself. Please call the station later to inquire about her whereabouts."

Mother kept rubbing her head as if she had a headache while speaking with the policeman.

She said, "I will call to check on her later."

CHAPTER 51

Mother went back upstairs to the apartment. When she came in Jermaine began questioning her.

Jermaine asked mother what happened. He said, "what did you do to make her lose it like that?"

Mother said, "I didn't do anything to that damn girl. All I did was open the bathroom door and she began screaming at me."

Jermaine said "I don't believe that. You had to do something to make her act like that. What did you say?

Mother said, "I did not say anything to her, you know she's crazy. You know it doesn't take much for that damn girl to flip out."

Jermaine looked at his mom suspiciously. He knew his mom loved drama and he knew she said something, he just didn't know what.

Catherine was in the front listening to the conversation they were having. She could not believe how easy it was for her mother to stand there and lie. But she said not a word. She just listened and smiled.

A grin appeared on mother's face.

Catherine looked at her and shook her head.

Jermaine looked at her like she was crazy. He asked, "why are you smiling?"

Mother said with a grin on her face "I did find out that the girl is pregnant."

Jermaine was shocked. His eyes nearly jumped out of his head.

Mother continued, "When I opened the door on her, she was about to put on her clothes. That's when I saw the bulge in her stomach. She has been hiding it. I knew something was going on with her."

Jermaine held his head down and started shaking it. He said, "you are going to get enough of butting into people's business. I knew you did something."

Mother said, "I didn't do anything to that crazy ass girl. It's not my fault that she went and got herself pregnant."

Jermaine said "If I was her I would have hidden it too. You are not the kind of mother that you can share things with. You're just as crazy as she is."

Mother said, "she was going to have to bring the little bastard home eventually. What was she going to do with it when she had it?"

Jermaine did not know what to think about the situation. He was sad for Tabatha going to the crazy house. He had no idea what was going to happen next.

Mother continued smiling and shaking her head.

She could not believe that Tabatha attacked her. She knew she had a mean streak, but this was on a whole other level.

CHAPTER 52

Mother decided to check on Tabatha at the crazy hospital. She wanted to find out how long they were going to keep her there.

When she arrived, she was told that the doctor wanted to see her first before she could see Tabatha.

Mother was directed into the doctor's office by the nurse. When mother got into the office, she questioned the doctor.

She asked, "why did I have to come in here to see you?"

The doctor responded, "I needed to ask you some questions in regard to Tabatha."

Mother said with an attitude, "let's make it quick, I have things to do. Shoot!"

The doctor asked, "what happened on the day that Tabatha was brought here?"

Mother responded, "the girl attacked me."

The doctor continued, "do you know why that happened?"

Mother said, "No! Did you ask her why she attacked me?"

The doctor said, "Yes! But she does not want to go into details about it."

Mother said, "nothing happened to her, all I did was open the bathroom door on her, and she went into a rage."

The doctor asked, "why do you think she went into a rage?"

Mother responded while smirking, "I think it's because I found out that she was pregnant."

The doctor continued, "why would that be a problem?"

The smirk left her face. Mother asked, "why are you asking me all of these questions? You need to be asking her crazy ass. What do I look like, a mind reader? All I know is you all better give her something to calm her crazy ass down, because she may not make it to the hospital the next time."

The doctor looked at her with a puzzled expression. He did not ask her another question.

Mother asked, "is there anything else you want to ask doc? If not, can I go see my daughter?"

The doctor told mother that he did not have any more questions for her. He told her that it was alright for her to go.

When mother arrived at Tabatha's room, she looked through the glass window of the door. She was trying to see what mood the girl may have been in. All she saw was Tabatha lying in the bed.

Mother opened the door slowly.

Tabatha turned her head towards the door to see who was coming in. When she saw that it was mother, she just rolled her eyes and turned her head back the other way.

Mother walked towards her bed. She said, "hello."

Tabatha did not answer her.

Mother asked, "are you ok?"

Tabatha turned her whole body the opposite of where her mother stood.

Mother said, "I spoke to the doctor already and they should be letting you out of here soon."

Tabatha said nothing.

Mother became angry. She did not like the way Tabatha was treating her. So, she said "if you keep this shit up, I will make sure you stay in here longer. Hell, I think you and that little bastard of yours both need mental help."

Tabatha turned towards mother quickly.

Mother jumped back a little.

Tabatha gave her mother a look that sent chills through her body.

She felt like jumping up and smashing her face in. But she knew that she had to hold the fury in and play it off in this hospital.

She knew if she had said or done anything to mother, the doctor would not let her go home. And she wanted out of there in the worst way.

Mother stepped back a few paces and said "well, I'll see you when you get out."

Mother left the room quickly. She knew that she had to watch herself around Tabatha when she got out. She did not want a repeat of what happened last time.

CHAPTER 53

A few weeks later Tabatha came home.

The children were very happy to see her and greeted her with a hug.

Catherine saw Tabatha walking down the hallway of the doorway. She smiled a bit and said, hey; she did not want Tabatha to see that she was happy that she was back home.

Jermaine was sitting in the kitchen when Tabatha arrived. He got up out of his seat and walked over towards her. He said with a smile on his face "hey you! How are you feeling?"

Tabatha turned and looked up at him. She said, "I am fine."

Jermaine continued, "I know that you have been through a lot these few months. Mother told me that you were pregnant. I just can't understand why you didn't tell me."

Tabatha said, "I didn't tell anyone. I saw how you all treated Catherine, and I just didn't want any part of that."

Jermaine said, "that's different! Catherine being pregnant is different from you and you know that."

Tabatha asked, "how is it different and how would I know that?"

Jermaine said, "come on now. You know that there has always been a difference between Catherine and everyone else. You know that she's looked at as an outsider in this family. You know that we were taught that a long time ago. I think this pregnancy has affected your mind."

Tabatha was angered by what Jermaine had just said. She knew they did things to get Catherine in trouble, but this was something altogether new. She could not believe her ears. She could not believe that he felt there was a difference.

Jermaine continued with a smile on his face, "now, is there anything that I can do for you?"

Tabatha just kept staring at him. She said "Jermaine! What the hell is wrong with you? Why would you think that there's a difference between me and Catherine being pregnant? I know we did things to get her in trouble with mother, but this is different. We are both in the same boat here. I can't believe that you said that to me. Wow! This family is so fucked up."

Jermaine said with a strong voice, "what the hell is wrong with you? You act like something has changed about the way that I feel about that whore. She still don't mean shit to me. I know you are going through something while you're carrying that baby, so you may be a little messed up in the head. But ain't nothing changed about the way that I feel about that little bitch."

Tabatha was shocked for some reason. She never had any love for Catherine before, but something within her had changed. She was too tired to get into an argument with him right now. So, she just turned and started walking towards her room.

Jermaine said, "if you need anything, just let me know."

Tabatha continued walking, saying nothing.

When she entered the bedroom, she closed the door behind her.

Bernadette came into the room behind Tabatha.

She said "I am so happy that you are back home. Do you need me to help you with anything?"

Tabatha said "No! I just want to lie down for a little while."

Bernadette said with a smile "ok sis! But if you need anything, just let me know."

Bernadette was so excited because she had two sisters who were pregnant. She just wanted to make sure that she helped them both out as much as she could.

CHAPTER 54

Catherine heard a knock at the door. She went to answer it. When she opened the door, it was John.

Her eyes bucked and her heart skipped a beat. She did not want anyone to know about him.

She asked in a soft voice, "what are you doing here John? I told you that I would call you and meet you."

John said, "I waited for your call, but you never called me. I needed to see you. I want to make sure that my family was alright."

Catherine was very irritated. She said, "I told you to never come to my house."

John said, "I know, but I was worried about you. It's been over a week since I saw you last."

Catherine said, "But I told you never to come to my house."

John said, "look baby, I know what you told me. But we have not seen each other in over a week. Now, you can be mad at me all you want, or you can show me some love."

Catherine pushed John away from the door. She said, "meet me at your cousin's house. Give me a few and I will be there. Ok?"

John said ok, but he did not understand her reaction to seeing him. He went to his cousin's house and waited for her.

John had a lot of questions running through his head. He wondered why Catherine did not want him to come to her house. He also wondered why it seemed like she was always hiding him from her folks.

He said to himself (now, she goes to my house anytime she wants. But I can't come to hers. She's met just about everyone in my family, but I can't meet one of hers. Something had to give on this one. If I can show the world that I love her, I think she should do the same for me).

Catherine arrived at John's cousin's house an hour later.

John was very irritated by now. He asked, "what took you so long? You just live next door!"

Catherine responded "I had to make sure that no one saw you come to my house. You need to understand the situation. If my family found out about you, it will be hell to pay."

John looked at Catherine with a frown on his face.

Catherine continued, "I wish I could make you understand. John, you don't want them in your business. You don't want them to be any part of your life. I wish they were not part of my life."

John said "I have introduced you to almost everyone in my family. I just don't understand why you insist on hiding me."

Catherine said, "In order for us to be together, I have to hide you for now.

My people are different from yours. When the time comes, I will introduce you to them. And make sure you remember this day because you wanted to meet them."

John said, "I will wait for a while, but this will not continue. What's good for you shall be good for me. We are going to be together no matter what."

Catherine said under her breath, "boy, you just don't know."

John asked Catherine what she had said.

Catherine said, "nothing, you are right."

CHAPTER 55

John told Catherine to come closer to him. When she did, he gave her a big hug and kiss. He asked if she and the baby were feeling alright. He rubbed her belly while talking with her.

Catherine loved it when he did that. It made her feel so loved. Everything about John made her feel special. This was the first time in her life that she knew she had someone to count on and she was not going to let anyone take it away.

John asked, "are you coming home with me today? I will be off for a couple of days.

Catherine said, "yes, just let me go get some things to take with me.

Catherine went back to the apartment to get some things. She was stopped at the end of the hall by mother.

Mother was drunk again.

Mother said, "where in the hell are you going in such a hurry?"

Catherine said, "move out the way mother, I have something to do."

Mother moved every time Catherine moved. She said "you ain't going nowhere. You better go sit your pregnant ass down somewhere. You are too grown for your own good."

Catherine just looked up at mother.

Mother was making her very angry.

Catherine wanted to hit her. She knew it would not take much to knock her down because she was drunk. But Catherine could not bring herself to do it.

Mother said, "come on, move me out the way if you dare. Come on, you think you are so bad."

Mother stepped across the hall a little too fast, which made her stumble and fall over.

Catherine began laughing and walked fast to her room.

Mother started screaming in a drunken voice, "BRING YOUR LITTLE ASS BACK HERE. YOU THINK SHIT FUNNY. I'LL SHOW YOU!"

Catherine's younger sister and brother came out of the room when mother was screaming. They went over to help her up off the floor.

Mother said, "leave me the fuck alone. Get away from me."

But they continued trying to help her get up.

Catherine gathered her things as fast as she could. When she was done, she walked back towards the door. She looked down at her mother and began laughing again. She turned towards the door a left while laughing.

Mother was pissed. She screamed, "DON'T BRING YOUR FAT NASTY ASS BACK HERE ANYMORE!"

CHAPTER 56

Catherine met John back at his cousin's house. They went down the back way of the building to his car. She kept looking around to make sure that no one saw them leaving.

John said, "you act like we're thieves or something. The way you keep looking around, you make us look suspicious. This just doesn't make any sense at all to me."

Catherine said, "in time you will understand, but now is not the time. Let's go!"

They got into the car and went to John's house. When they arrived, the first person to greet them was John's dad.

John's dad's face had a huge smile on it.

It kind of creeped Catherine out, but she smiled back and said hello.

John did not like that his dad was all in Catherine's face.

When he looked at his dad, he frowned and walked towards his bedroom. He grabbed Catherine's hand and pulled her to follow him.

Catherine smiled while John was pulling her. She just walked, wobbling behind him.

Catherine began putting her things down and looked over at John. He seemed frustrated. She wondered what was wrong with him.

She went over to him and hugged him.

She asked, "what's wrong? You look like something is on your mind."

John said, "nothing is wrong. I just can't wait until I get out of here."

Catherine was shocked. She said, "get out of here. Are you crazy? You don't know how good you got it. You live in a house and you're still not happy. What's wrong with you? I think we need to switch places so that you can see what you have."

John said, "you don't know what you're talking about. You only see this house. You don't know the things that go on here. I can't wait until I get my own place."

Catherine said, "from what I see, I would choose this than going back to my place.

I don't see your doors opening and closing all day long. I don't see people trying to hurt one another either. You can come home and go to your room, and nobody bothers you. So, what in the world are you talking about? Why would you rush to leave such peace? I wish for one day that I could live like this."

John said, "girl, you better be careful of what you ask for. You don't know everything about my family, and you don't want to know. I guess as we grow closer, I will let you in on some details of the history of this family. But for now, just trust me when I say we have to get our own place as soon as possible."

Catherine said OK and rolled her eyes.

She could not understand where John was coming from.

She didn't understand the way he thought, but for now, she was going to let it go. She also knew that she had better not say anything to John about his dad giving her money.

So, she just focused on getting all the attention from John.

Catherine asked John for another hug. She always felt a little safer when she was in his arms.

John held her tight. He did not squeeze too tight because she was so big now.

He asked if she was hungry and went to fix her something to eat.

When John arrived in the kitchen, he saw his mom.

John said, "hey mom, I didn't know you were home."

John's mom asked, "where else would I be?"

John said "I don't know! Because I didn't see you when I came in, I thought you were gone."

John's mom said, "nope, I've been right here all the time. I didn't hear you come in either. When did you get back in town?"

John said, "I just got back today, but before I came home, I went to get Catherine."

John's mom kind of frowned when she heard that Catherine was there.

John was surprised to see his mom's reaction to Catherine being there. He asked "what wrong with your face mom?"

John's mom didn't even notice that she had frowned. She said, "nothing! Why did you ask that?"

John said, "when I told you that Catherine was here, a frown appeared on your face. Do you have a problem with Catherine being here?"

John's mom said, "no son, I don't have a problem with Catherine being here at all. I can't even tell you why that happened."

John's mom was very careful of what she said to John. She knew that he was very protective of Catherine. But internally, she had a slight problem with Catherine being there, because she saw the way that her husband looked at her all the time. She knew that she could not share this with John. She decided to just wait to see how things may play out.

John was a little skeptical about accepting his mom's answer, but he decided to let it go because he had to fix Catherine something to eat.

John's father came into the kitchen and spoke.

John instantly got an attitude, just from the presence of his father.

John's father said, "we're not speaking today, son?"

John said Hey and kept doing what he was doing.

John's father asked, "what are we cooking today?"

John responded, "I am fixing Catherine something to eat."

John's mom said, "honey, if you are hungry, your food is in the oven."

John's father said, "no, I'm not hungry. I just wanted to see what he was cooking. I was just trying to talk with my son. But I see there is no need for that because someone has a little chip on his shoulder."

John was aggravated. He knew that his dad was trying to get something started. So, he decided to ignore him as much as he could.

John's mom looked at both of them. She knew that John was aggravated and that her husband was trying to bait him into an argument.

She said, "everything is alright honey. If you need me to bring you your lunch, just let me know."

John's father continued looking at John with his eyes squinted. He let out a low grunt and walked out of the kitchen.

While he was walking out, he said, "people need to know their place in this house. They better start respecting their elders or there are going to be some problems here."

John's father walked towards the bedroom. He looked in on Catherine.

When he looked in the room, he saw Catherine lying down.

Catherine was a little startled to see John's father looking in the room.

She said, "hello".

John's father just smiled, in a Chester the molester way. You could see that he had something up his sleeves.

He said, "hey baby girl. How have you been feeling?"

Catherine said, "ok, a little slower that's all."

John's dad asked, "do you need anything? Do you need more money?"

Catherine became nervous. She knew John was not far from the room and she did not want him to hear what his father was saying.

Catherine said, "you'd better gone with that. If John hears you talking like that it won't be good for either one of us. He does not know that you give me money. He doesn't know that you come by my house from time to time. I thank you for helping me out when John is gone, but he does not want me bothering with you at all. So, gone with that stuff, before you get us both in trouble.

John's dad just smiled and said, "as you wish! But if you need anything, you know you can count on me."

Catherine nodded her head and waved her hands to shoo him off. Catherine knew that he was up to something.

She put him in the same category of the other men in the building that she messes with. She knew he was up to no good, but she was going to make the best of the situation while she could.

CHAPTER 57

John's mom looked at John with a heartfelt look and said, "don't worry about that baby, you know how your father gets."

John was furious and said in a low voice "I am tired of this stuff mom. He's always trying to start something with me. I can't wait until I'm able to get out of here.

John saw the way that his dad looked at Catherine. He saw that his dad made it a point to be in her face every time she came over. But he knew he could not share this information with his mom.

John's mom said, "I know, I know, but you know your father."

John said in a smart tone, "but you know him too."

John's mom was taken back a little by his tone. She asked, "what do you mean by that John?"

John held his head down. He did not mean to lash out at his mom.

He said, "sorry mom, I meant nothing by that. Dad just frustrates me so much."

John's mom said, "why don't you go back in the room with Catherine? I will finish cooking for you all. Don't worry about nothing son, everything will be alright."

John said thanks to his mom, but what his father just did was still on his mind.

John wanted to come up with a plan as soon as possible to get out of his parent's house. He knew that it would not be long before he and his father would get into it about Catherine.

He knew his father was up to no good, but the way his father was acting now showed him that he needed to be prepared for anything. This man had something on his mind and seemed like he was about to put it into play.

CHAPTER 58

When John went back to the room, he found Catherine sitting up. She looked like she had something on her mind.

John said, "hey you, what's wrong."

Catherine shook her head and said nothing.

John said, "it looks like you got something on your mind."

Catherine was not about to tell him what had just happened between her and his father.

Catherine said, "all I have on my mind right now is eating. Where is my food you went to make?"

John said, "my mom is finishing up everything for us. I had to get out of that kitchen for a minute."

Catherine asked, "why? What happened in the kitchen?

John said, "don't worry about it, I will tell you later. Let's just get something in our stomachs."

John's mom announced that the food was done. Catherine and John went to the kitchen table and began to eat.

The way Catherine was eating, you would have thought that you had found her homeless off the streets. She was tearing that food up. She left no prisoners.

After they finished eating, they both went back into the room and took a nap.

While they were sleeping, John's dad peeped through the door watching them sleep. He did not hear his wife walking up behind him.

She said, "what are you doing?"

John's dad was startled for a minute. He said, "don't be sneaking up behind me. I ain't doing nothing. I was just checking on them to see if they needed anything."

John's mom said, "They're sleeping and you know it. Why are watching her so much?"

John's dad said, "what are you talking about. I'm not watching her. I told you I was checking on them to see if they needed anything."

John's mom said, "well, now you see that they are asleep get away from the door."

John's dad said, "you'd better watch who you are talking to like that. You don't tell me what to do, this is my house, and I can go where I please. I don't have to answer you or no one else in this house. This is my house and don't you forget it."

John's mom just shook her head at him. She said, "still, get away from that door before your son sees you."

John's dad walked towards the living room and mom followed behind him.

John's dad became angry. He said, "what, you think I'm scared of my son?"

John's mom said, "no honey! You just don't want him to jump to the wrong conclusions. That's all I'm saying."

John's dad said, "I wouldn't care what he thought if he saw me at the door. Like I said, this is my house, and I have to answer to no one. Remember that!"

John's dad went and got his jacket and walked out of the house. He needed to get his thoughts together now that he's kind of been caught. He had to find a way to get the attention off him. He didn't mean to make watching her so noticeable. I guess he got comfortable because Catherine was taking some of his generosity.

He wondered if she thought the same way that his wife and son did. If she did, it would throw a wrench in his plans. He had to change his plans and the way that he thought as fast as possible. No one could be on to him because it would cause a huge problem.

John's mom stood there in the living room for a moment after her husband left. She was a bit concerned about his actions. She had a feeling that things were about to go from bad to worse. She did not know what to do to prevent what she thought was coming. So, she decided to pray about and leave it in God's hands.

CHAPTER 59

Catherine and John woke up from their nap.

John had to take Catherine back home because he had to go to work the next day. This time the trip was going to take about three to four days to complete.

Catherine was disappointed because she wanted to stay longer. She hated going back home sometimes because it was always some stuff going on. She felt like she had not been gone long enough to get the energy to deal with her family.

Catherine asked John if there was any way that she could stay a little longer.

John said, "you can't stay. I have to go to work tomorrow."

Catherine said. "please John, I am not ready to go back home yet. Is there anything I could do for you to let me stay?"

John said, "no baby, I'm sorry. There is no way that I would leave you here while I am gone."

Catherine asked, why? She said, "you could trust me. Nothing is going to happen while you are gone."

John said, "I just don't want you here without me. I will be gone longer this time, so there is no need for you to be here."

Catherine said, "I only get rest when I am here with you. I need all the rest that I can get."

John said, "I know you need your rest, but there is nothing I can do about it right now. I have to go to work. I have things that I have to do. Soon you will be able to rest as much as you need. No one is going to be bothering you soon."

Catherine was sad and still tired. She wished he would change his mind, but he didn't.

John told Catherine to get her things and they left his parents' house. They barely said anything to one another on the way home.

Catherine just sat back with her head turned the opposite way of John.

John said, "please, don't be mad at me. You have to trust me when I say I can't leave you there by yourself."

Catherine was irritated. She said, "what do you think is going to happen? Is someone going to kill me or something? Well hell, let them come do it. Anything is better than going back to my apartment."

John laughed a bit. He said, "don't be stupid. No one is going to hurt you at my house."

Catherine snapped again. She said, "so, now I'm stupid."

John's smile left his face.

Catherine continued in a louder voice "so, now I'm stupid. I am not stupid by a long shot. You think you know me, you don't. I've been taking care of myself for a long time. I'm not stupid and I'm not going to let you or anyone else call me stupid."

John said with a nervous voice, "I didn't call you stupid. I just said that what you said, was stupid."

Catherine said, "yeah, I heard you."

John said, "no, that's not what I meant. Come on Catherine, don't twist my words."

Catherine said, "I ain't twisting shit. That's what came out of your mouth. You think I'm stupid and I'm not good enough to stay at your house by myself."

John said, "no I don't. I don't think you're stupid. I have my reasons for not wanting you to stay at my house. I can't make you understand right now, but you will later."

John pulled up to Catherine's building. She got out without kissing him. He got out of the car to follow her. She told him to stop.

Catherine said in a sarcastic voice, "I don't need you walking me anywhere. You can go now."

John said, "come on, don't be like that."

Catherine continued walking to the building.

John said, "I'll call you later!"

Catherine turned and said, "don't bother!"

She turned and went to the elevator.

John did not know what else to do, so he left.

He knew that he had to work on his plan soon. He had to make some moves that he was not prepared to do. He felt like he was about to lose Catherine and he was not going to let that happen.

He could not tell her about his thoughts about his father. She did not know him like he did. He believed she would not understand where he was coming from. All he knew was that he had to get them away from his parents as soon as possible.

John arrived at the house after dropping Catherine off. He started packing for the trip. He had to leave early that next morning.

He made a couple of phone calls before he went to bed. The response to the phone calls made him incredibly happy.

John was in good spirits knowing that everything was about to come together sooner than expected. With all that information, it did not take him long to go to sleep.

CHAPTER 60

Catherine opened the door to her apartment. When she came in, there were people all over the place. She didn't know what was going on.

The first person to see Catherine was Bernadette. She said, "girl, mother is having another party."

Catherine asked, "for what?"

Bernadette responded, "no reason! She said she just felt like partying."

Catherine said, "mother always had a reason for doing things. Nothing that she does just happens."

Catherine walked and looked around the house. People were smoking, drinking, and playing cards and dominos while the music was playing and most of the people there were men.

She wondered what her mother had up her sleeves.

Catherine began walking down the hall to her bedroom. Jermaine was walking towards her.

He said, "hey, little bitch. I see you found your way back home."

Catherine did not feel like dealing with him right now.

Jermaine continued, "oh, you can't talk now. I heard you had a lot of shit to say before you left."

Catherine said, "boy, I don't know what you are talking about."

Jermaine said with a smug tone, "so now you don't know what I'm talking about. Ok! Let me tell you this, if anyone says that anything smart came out of your mouth again, I will be to see ya."

Catherine was always on guard when Jermaine was around, she never felt safe around him. She continued looking at him passing by her and went into her room.

CHAPTER 61

Tabatha was in the bed lying down, she looked very irritated.

Catherine spoke to Tabatha and asked how she was feeling.

Tabatha said, "hey! Where have you been?

Catherine was surprised by the question. Tabatha never cared if she was there or gone.

Catherine said, "I've just been out. Why? What's wrong?"

Tabatha said, "nothing, I was just asking. She turned back on her side."

Suddenly things just went quiet. Then Tabatha slowly turned back over.

Tabatha asked, "why do you keep leaving me here alone?"

Catherine responded, "what?"

Tabatha said, "you heard me. Why do you keep leaving me here alone?"

Catherine was taken back for a moment.

She said to herself, "this girl is really going through it. Why is she asking these crazy questions? She's never cared one way or the other if I was dead or alive. Let me just catch myself and try to understand her condition.

Catherine said in a calm voice "Tabatha, I did not leave you. We have never too much been around each other."

Tabatha said, "it doesn't matter. When you are gone, they focus on me. I can't take this shit anymore. I can't sleep. I can barely eat without throwing up. Mother keeps calling me lazy. Jermaine keeps calling me crazy and Bernadette is just a little too helpful for me. She makes my stomach queasy. And on top of all that, they keep asking me who the daddy is."

Catherine was offended. She said, "how did you get from all of that, that I keep leaving you?"

Tabatha said, "if you didn't leave so much, things would go back to the way they were."

Catherine said, "WHAT? You mean to tell me, that your problems with mother and them, is because I'm not here?"

Tabatha said with a straight face, "Yeah! If you were here the focus would not be on me so much. I thought that I was going to get through this pregnancy without them being on my back. But no, you had to find a way to get your ass up out of here anytime you want."

Catherine was pissed. She could not believe what she was hearing. She thought to herself, "this fucking family is crazy. This bitch thinks that I am going to be the scape goat for her. She would rather they fuck with me than her. Pregnancy did not change her one bit, she's still the same selfish stuck-up bitch that she always was).

Catherine said with a smirk on her face, "what's that saying you use to always say to me? Let me think for a moment. Oh yeah, better you than me."

Tabatha's face turned red. But it was nothing she could do to Catherine at this time. She was too sickly, big, and slow. The pregnancy was wearing her out. She just looked at Catherine like she wanted to kill her.

Catherine continued to smile and then left the room.

CHAPTER 62

While she was coming out of the room, a couple of guys passed by. They spoke to her, but one of them smacked her on her behind and laughed about it. She rubbed it for a few minutes and turned back around walking to the front.

She saw Jermaine conversing with some of the guests. He seemed to be having a grand old time.

When Jermaine saw Catherine coming down the hall his facial expression changed immediately.

Catherine saw the way Jermaine's face changed. She did not know what was wrong with him and she was not about to try and find out. She decided to keep her distance and began mingling with some of the guys there.

Jermaine continued following her with his eyes. It seemed like the more he watched her, the angrier he got.

He hated the way she smiled and laughed. He hated seeing the men there pay her so much attention. He did not understand what they saw in her while she was pregnant. The whole thing made him sick to his stomach.

Catherine was so caught up in her conversations that she paid him no mind. She was having a good old time with the guests there. She was even happier when she put the food that was laid out in her mouth.

Jermaine could not take his eyes off her, so he asked one of the guys there to leave with him so they could go smoke. He could not take seeing Catherine anymore.

He needed to get away and clear his mind from all of the chaos that was going on in his mind.

Jermaine's friend asked what was wrong with him while they were smoking.

Jermaine said, "Nothing man, I just get tired of seeing her sometimes."

His friend asked, "seeing who?"

Jermaine responded, "Catherine! I can't stand her presence sometimes. I can't stand seeing her face, smile, nor that belly of hers with that bastard in there."

His friend shook his head and continued passing the joint.

Jermaine had really bad thoughts about Catherine. He even imagined killing her one day. Just her being able to walk around in his presence upset him in a way that no brother should feel about his sister.

Jermaine's anger inside of him spilled out as if he were possessed by some unnatural being. If anyone could read his thoughts, their soul would shiver. There was something sadistic about his emotions toward Catherine.

The more he thought about her the more he became angry. He started pacing the floor faster and faster while puffing on the shared joint. He had completely lost himself in his thoughts.

His friend said, "dude, what's with you today? You are straight tripping."

Jermaine just looked up at him. His eyes were red now.

His friend was caught off guard by the way his eyes looked. He said with hesitation, "I'm a talk with you later Jermaine. I have to make a run.

Jermaine's friend did not like the look on his face, so he decided to get away from him before anything happened. He had seen Jermaine's temper before.

Jermaine did not respond to his friend, he just kept walking back and forth.

CHAPTER 63

Catherine loved eating, especially now that she was pregnant. It did not matter what it was, as long as it tasted good, it was in her mouth.

Even though she constantly ate, she did not get that big. She was still a little old cute thing and the men confirmed that with the attention they continued to show her.

The attention was well received by Catherine. It made her feel great at times and other times it got on her nerves.

The best attention that she got came from John. All he had to do was smile and it would melt Catherine's insides. When he talked, it made her want to dive on him. Everything about this man sent a warm fuzzy feeling throughout her body.

Catherine had never felt things like this before. Even though it was scary at times, she looked forward to experiencing it each time she could.

Catherine was in some kind of love, and she made sure that no one in her family would take that away from her. He was hers and no one there would ever experience him if she could help it.

Catherine came out of her thoughts about John and continued mingling with the guests. She saw her mom living it up sitting in her man's lap while drinking and smoking.

Chapter 64

Bernadette and George were running back and forth because mother kept kicking them out. The party was no place for the young ones.

Everything seemed to be going fine with the party.

Mother always gave great parties no matter what. People were laughing, talking, dancing, playing cards, dominos, and drinking. Everything was going just fine until Jermaine came back into the apartment lunging at Catherine.

Everyone was caught off guard at the site of Jermaine attacking Catherine.

No words had transpired, he just came in with this look on his face searching for his target. When he found her, he went towards her quickly and grabbed her by the throat.

Catherine did not know what was happening. She did not see him coming. All she could do was grab his hands that were around her neck. She tried pulling them off, but he was too strong for her.

Jermaine's veins were popping out of his forehead, while he was tightening his grasp on her.

Catherine began going down to the floor. She was gasping for air while pulling on his hands trying to free herself.

Everyone at the party was shocked at the site.

Mother's boyfriend pushed her off his lap and ran towards Jermaine and Catherine.

A couple of other men ran over too, so they could help get Jermaine off Catherine.

Mother's boyfriend was screaming at Jermaine, while trying to get him off her, "LET HER GO JERMAINE! LET HER GO!"

Jermaine's eyes were so red. All you could see was hate in them. He didn't look at anyone else but Catherine. He was completely focused on what he intended to do.

The men could not get him to let go of his grip on her, so one of the guys punched him in the face. This sent him tumbling across the floor.

Mother's boyfriend grabbed Catherine and lifted her up and carried her to the back.

She was gasping for air while coughing. She continued holding and rubbing her neck. She was still shocked by what had happened.

Once Jermaine got his bearings, he began to jump up screaming "WHO IN THE HELL HIT ME?"

One of the men said, call down man. You can't do that to that girl."

Jermaine yelled "GET THE FUCK OUT OF MY WAY. I'M GOING TO KILL HER!"

The men ran towards him and grabbed him.

He was screaming "I AM GOING TO KILL THAT BITCH! WHERE IS SHE?"

He gave them one hell of a fight.

Jermaine was not a weak man; he was strong as an ox. It took more men to help hold him down. He was like a madman; like something had taken over him. It was like he was possessed by evil demons or something.

One of the guys holding Jermaine screamed at him asking "MAN, WHAT THE HELL IS WRONG WITH YOU? WHY WOULD YOU DO THAT TO YOUR SISTER?

Jermaine continued screaming "GET YOUR MOTHERFUCKING HANDS OFF OF ME! THIS DON'T HAVE SHIT TO DO WITH YOU!"

The men paid him no attention and kept holding him. They were not going to let him go until he calmed down.

Mother came over and stood over him while the guys were holding him. She said "you just have to keep messing up everything. You are one sorry ass boy. That girl ain't did nothing to you. What the hell is wrong with you Jermaine? What is it about Catherine that drives you mad? You don't act like this towards nobody else."

Jermaine looked up at her and said "Don't come asking me shit! Take your raggedy ass on somewhere and sit your motherfuckin ass down."

Mother looked at him and turned to go towards the kitchen. When she returned to Jermaine, she had her broom in her hand.

The men said "please, don't hit him. We got him!"

Mother paid them no attention. She looked down at Jermaine and said, "I told you about talking to me like that" and started swinging the broom stick at him.

The guys had to let Jermaine go, because they did not want to get hit.

Jermaine was trying to duck and grab the broom.

Mother continued swinging until she made contact with Jermaine's head. When she made contact, all you saw was blood splattering everywhere.

Jermaine yelled with agony and grabbed his head.

Mother continued swinging and made contact again. This time she hit him on the back of his head, and it started bleeding too.

The men ran and grabbed her, so that she could stop swinging the broom.

Mother was so scarily calm while everything was going on.

Jermaine was cursing and holding his head and then he fell to the floor. A couple of guys ran over to him. One of the guys told someone to call an ambulance, while he was trying to help stop the bleeding.

Everyone was shocked by the amount of blood that was pouring from his head, so people began leaving.

The guy holding Jermaine's head said, "someone get me a towel so I can place it on his head to stop the bleeding."

No one moved, they kept looking at the blood pouring out of Jermaine's head.

The guy started screaming "SOMEONE GET ME A DAMN TOWEL FOR HIS HEAD!"

A woman ran over to mother and asked where the towels were.

Mother was standing there looking in space. She did not respond to the woman.

The woman grabbed her and shook her a little and asked again.

Mother pushed the woman off her. She said "what the hell is wrong with you? You better get your hands off me."

The woman said "I mean you no disrespect. I'm just trying to get a towel for your son's head. Please tell me where you keep the towels."

Mother said, let that fool bleed to death, you are not going to mess up my towels.

Everyone was shocked by her response. They didn't know what to say.

George ran to the front and gave the man a towel for Jermaine's head.

Mother said "get yo lil ass back in your room. Didn't nobody tell you to do nothing.

Take yo ass back in that room before I slap the piss out of you."

George ran back before mother got a hold of him.

CHAPTER 65

Mother's boyfriend was still in the bedroom with Catherine. He laid her down on the bed and asked if she needed anything.

Catherine was still trying to breathe normally; she was still coughing and gaging.

Tabatha woke up from hearing all the commotion. She asked, "what's going on?"

Mother's boyfriend said, "Jermaine tried to kill this girl."

Tabatha jumped up from the bed. She could not believe what she had just heard. She said, "what did you just say?"

Mother's boyfriend said, "your brother Jermaine, tried to kill your sister."

Tabatha began rubbing her head while looking down at Catherine. She was trying to figure this thing out. Nothing added up for her, she had more questions.

Mother's boyfriend continued patting Catherine's back as she coughed. He asked her if she wanted a glass of water.

Catherine said yes with a soft voice.

Tabatha asked Catherine if she was alright.

She said, "girl, you and Jermaine need to cut this stuff out. What did you all get into it about now?

Catherine looked at Tabatha like she was crazy. She was not able to speak yet, so she just frowned a little.

Tabatha continued "You better quit messing with that fool, he gone mess around and kill you. You know it don't take much to set him off."

Catherine said in a soft voice, "I didn't do anything to him."

Tabatha could barely hear her. She said, "what did you say?"

Catherine tried speaking louder but was unable to.

Mother's boyfriend came back in with the water. He gave it to her and asked if she needed anything else.

While drinking the water, Catherine shook her head no.

Tabatha asked Mother's boyfriend what happened. She told him that she had asked Catherine, but she could hardly hear her.

Mother's boyfriend told her that he didn't know what happened. He said, "Jermaine just came in the house walking fast towards Catherine. When he got to her, he grabbed her by the neck and began choking her."

Tabatha asked, "what happened before all of this occurred?"

Mother's boyfriend responded, "nothing, nothing happened that I saw. Everybody was mingling and having a good time. Catherine was laughing and talking with a couple of guys before he came in."

Tabatha said, "that does not make any sense. Why would Jermaine just come in out of the blue and attack her like that?"

Catherine called Mother's boyfriend like she was in pain.

Mother's boyfriend and Tabatha's head whipped towards her. He asked, "are you ok?"

Catherine said with pain in her voice 'I need to go to the doctor. Please help me get to the doctor."

Tabatha bent down and asked her what was hurting.

Catherine could hardly speak. She said in her painful voice "please, get me to the doctor." She continued holding her stomach.

Mother's boyfriend ran out of the room screaming "CALL THE AMBULANCE, SOMEONE CALL THE AMBULANCE. CATHERINE NEEDS TO GET TO THE HOSPITAL RIGHT AWAY. SHE'S IN A LOT OF PAIN."

CHAPTER 66

Mother's boyfriend didn't know that the ambulance was already there for Jermaine. He asked them to come check on Catherine because she was pregnant and in a lot of pain.

One of the attendants ran down the hall with Mother's boyfriend to check on Catherine. When they got to the bedroom, they heard her screaming. They opened the door fast. They saw her holding her stomach while tears rolled down her face.

Tabatha was trying to comfort her, but there was nothing she could do to help the pain go away.

The attendant put his hand on her head to see if she had a fever. Then he grabbed her wrist and asked how far along she was.

Catherine could hardly speak, so Tabatha told the attendant how far along she was.

The attendant continued checking her vital signs. He said that Catherine was about to give birth. He got up and called for the other attendant.

The other attendant could not leave Jermaine, so he told someone to call for another ambulance.

The attendant that was with Catherine was trying to coach her with her breathing. He told her that she had to calm down and try taking deep breaths.

Catherine was in so much pain. She did not know what to do. She had never felt pain like this before. She continued moaning and grabbing her stomach.

Tabatha was looking around in disbelief. She was surprised by what the attendant had said. She thought that it was too soon for Catherine to have her baby. She did not know what to do, so she just stood around and watched everything that was going on.

The attendant was trying to gain Tabatha's attention. He needed her to help him with Catherine. He kept saying, "miss, oh miss. Excuse me miss."

Tabatha did not respond, she just kept looking and listening to everything that was going on.

The attendant stopped trying to call her and grabbed her by her pant leg.

Tabatha nearly jumped out of her skin. She said, "why are you grabbing my pants?"

The attendant said, "I need your help miss. I tried getting your attention by calling you, but you did not respond."

Tabatha said, "what is it that you want?"

The attendant said, "I need you to go to the front and see if anyone called for more help."

Tabatha ran out the door to the front and asked if anyone called for more help.

When mother saw her, she said, "what's going on back there?

Tabatha told her mother that she thinks Catherine was about to have her baby. She said, "the attendant told me to come up here to see if anyone called for more help because he needs to get her to the hospital as soon as he could."

Mother said, "you all are acting like a woman had never had a child at home before. You all are making a big deal out of nothing. She could stay her little ass right here and have that damn baby."

One of the guys there answered Tabatha saying that he had called for another ambulance, and they said they would be here in a few moments.

Tabatha turned from mother and looked down at Jermaine. The other attendant was doing everything that he could to stop the bleeding of Jermaine's head. The sight of all that blood began to make Tabatha feel sick and sad. All she could do was cover her mouth and shake her head in disbelief.

Tabatha turned from Jermaine and went back into the room and told the attendant that someone had called, and they would be there soon.

Suddenly Catherine screamed. The screech scared everyone in the room.

The attendant told Catherine to try turning onto her back. He told her that he needed to check her cervix to see if the baby was coming.

Catherine was still holding Mother's boyfriend's hand. He and the attendant had to help her roll onto her back.

The attendant went down to check to see if he saw the baby coming. He did not see the head of the baby, so he began to examine her cervix. He placed his hand inside her and found out that she had dilated six centimeters. He took his hand out of her and told her that she had to do everything she could to calm down or she was going to have the baby right now.

Catherine said in a pain-stricken voice, "I'm trying to calm down, but it hurts. Please help me, I can't take this pain." and she screamed again while crying.

Catherine's scream shook Tabatha to the core. She was scared out of her mind.

The attendant said, "stop screaming, you are going to hurt yourself and the baby. If you keep screaming, you are going to push this baby out before you are ready.

Catherine continued, "I'm trying, it hurts, it really hurts. Please help me Mr., Please help me." and she screamed again while squeezing Mother's boyfriend's hand.

The attendant went back down and checked her again, she was eight centimeters now. He got up and told Tabatha to go get some towels. He said that Catherine was about to have her baby right now.

Mother's boyfriend became extremely nervous. He didn't know what to do.

The attendant saw his face and told him to calm down. He said, "all I need for you to do is continue holding her hand. You are her support system."

Mother's boyfriend let out a strong sigh of relief. He said, "ok, I can do that."

Tabatha ran to the closet to gather up some towels. Before she could turn around, the other ambulance people arrived.

One ran back to the room and the other helped the other attendant get Jermaine onto the bed to take him to the hospital.

The attendants that were in the front left for the hospital. The other two were in the room with Catherine.

The attendants were trying to get Catherine to control her breathing. They told her that if she did not control her breathing, it would make the baby come sooner.

Catherine said while screaming, crying and breathing hard, "I'M TRYING, I'M TRYING, BUT IT HURTS SO BAD. PLEASE HELP ME, I FEEL LIKE I'M ABOUT TO DIE. I DON'T WANT TO DIE. PLEASE HELP ME."

One of the attendants told her that she had to calm down. He said, "we are not going to let anything bad happen to you. But you have to calm down for the sake of the child that you are carrying."

Catherine held Mother's boyfriend's hand tighter as another contraction came. She tried not to scream but was unable to hold it.

The attendants looked at each other with fear in their eyes. One told the other that they were not going to make it to the hospital. He said that she was about to give birth right there because she was beginning to crown.

The attendant told Catherine that she was about to have the baby.

Tabatha was in shock by everything that was going on. She couldn't move a muscle; she just stood there and watched everything.

Catherine screamed and moaned again.

The attendant told her that she was going to have to stop screaming. He said, "you are going to rip yourself if you continue to scream. You are going to make the baby come before your body is ready. Please, Catherine, listen to me and try harder to control your breathing."

Catherine said, "ok, I will try."

The attendant told Tabatha to get some blankets and hot water, but she did not move.

The attendant called out to her again, but she did not respond.

The attendant asked Mother's boyfriend to let go of Catherine's hand and run out there and ask for some blankets and hot water.

Catherine screamed "PLEASE DON'E LEAVE ME!" She held Mother's boyfriend's hand tighter.

Mother's boyfriend said nervously, "I am not going to leave you. I will be right back. I have to get these things for you so that they can help you. I will be right back I promise."

He ran out of the room yelling down the hall.

Catherine began to cry hysterically.

One of the attendants tried to calm her down. He spoke to her in such a caring voice that Catherine began to calm down.

He asked the other attendant if he was ready.

He shook his head signaling yes, with a look in his eyes saying that there was no more time.

He told Catherine that they could not wait any longer. He told her that she would have to sit up a little and the next time she felt pressure to push down as if she was about to have a bowel movement.

Catherine began to sit up and the pain came again. She began to push, and the baby came right out.

Tabatha saw the baby come out and fainted on the bed.

The attendant cleared out the mouth of the baby and it began to cry.

Catherine was relieved that the pain went away. She asked in a soft voice, "what is it?"

The attendant told her that it was a boy.

Catherine said, "oh wow, I had a boy. Oh wow, it's a boy." She smiled and began to think of John. She believed that John would be happy with the news that he had a son.

Mother's boyfriend came in with the water and a blanket. He saw that Catherine had had the baby already. He looked at Catherine and asked if she was ok and saw that Tabatha was sleeping on the bed.

The attendants began to clean the baby and wrapped him up in the blanket that Mother's boyfriend had given them. They gave the baby to Catherine and began covering her up so they could take them both to the hospital.

They put Catherine and the baby on the roll away bed and secured her. Before they began to leave, one of the attendants checked on Tabatha to make sure that she was alright.

He said that she was fine, so they left.

CHAPTER 67

After everything calmed down, mother went to check on Tabatha. She opened the bedroom door and saw that Tabatha was still sleeping, so she closed it back up.

No one knew that Tabatha went into premature labor when she fainted.

The next morning everyone woke up to Tabatha screaming. Everyone ran towards the room. Mother's boyfriend was the first to enter the room. He stopped in his tracks when he saw all the blood. Everyone else ran into the back of him.

Everyone was shocked by the sight of the blood. Mother's boyfriend ran over to her and asked if she was okay. He said, "what's wrong Tabatha, where did all this blood come from?"

Tabatha was too weak to respond, so all she did was hold her stomach and cry. She was rocking back and forward in the blood shaking her head back and forth.

Mother's boyfriend grabbed her by the hand and tried to pull her up, this made her scream again.

He yelled at mother and told her to get over there to help him pick her up and put her on the bed.

Mother just stood there like she was frozen.

Mother's boyfriend yelled at everyone telling them to go call 911. He said, "hurry up this, girl is in trouble.

He turned back to Tabatha and said, "tell me what you need so I can help you. Please,

Tabatha, you have to say something so that I can help you."

Tabatha was in so much pain, she was unable to speak. All she could do was hold her stomach and continue rocking back and forth.

She had never felt pain like this before, so she was unable to tell anyone what she needed.

Mother's boyfriend was the only one trying to help her. Everyone else just stood around like lost zombies.

No one knew how to act around all that blood. Shoot, the last time any one of them saw blood was when it was coming from Jermaine's head.

Mother finally came out of shock and said, "what the hell is going on with these kids? Everyone around here acting like they're dying or something. What, nobody around here can take a little pain? You had to experience some pain when your fast assess opened your legs for that dick to get in you.

Oh, Oh, so now it's different! You want to play like an adult when you lay on your back getting fucked and now you don't want to deal with the adult consequences. Shit, life is life, y'all made your beds now lie in that motherfucker."

Everyone looked up in shock at mother. They could not believe that she just said that.

Mother said, "what the fuck you looking at, did you think this was going to be anything different. These bitches go out and lay up with all these motherfucker's and get themselves pregnant and you want me to have sympathy. SHIT!!!!!"

Mother's boyfriend stood up and told her to get out of the room. He said, "as a matter of fact, everybody get the hell out."

Mother said, "who the fuck do you think you talking to? Motherfucker, this my house and you get up and get your raggedy ass up out of here. You don't run nothing up in here. You better quit running your fucking mouth before I mess around and crack your head open up in here."

Mother's boyfriend said, "why don't you take your dumb ass on somewhere and sit down.

This pissed mom off, so she began running toward him. She was calling him every name in the book while she was coming toward him. She had her arms stretched out running toward him ready to choke the shit out of him.

Mother's boyfriend braced for it and grabbed her so that she could not hit him.

He said, bitch calm the fuck down. Nobody got time for you acting a damn fool.

Mother was screaming, "LET ME GO BASTARD, GET YOUR DAMN HANDS OFF ME. YOU DON'T TALK TO ME LIKE THAT MOTHERFUCKER, YOU DON'T KNOW WHO YOU ARE PLAYING WITH."

Mother's boyfriend said yelling" THIS GIRL IS IN TROUBLE, SO, WE DON'T HAVE TIME

FOR THIS BULLSHIT YOU ARE PULLING RIGHT NOW. WHY DON'T YOU GO TAKE YOUR CRAZY ASS OUTSIDE AND LOOK TO SEE IF THE AMBULANCE IS COMING. CAN YOU DO THAT, CAN YOU JUST DO THAT SHIT RIGHT NOW?

Tabatha began screaming again and more blood started gushing out of her and she fell back on the bed.

Mother's boyfriend grabbed her and started shaking her. He was trying to get her to wake up, but she wouldn't. He got scared because he thought she had died.

The children began to cry and called out Tabatha's name.

The ambulance finally came and rushed right into the bedroom. The attendants asked what had happened.

Mother's boyfriend told them they had woken up to her screaming and when they came into the room she was sitting in blood.

The attendant put her on the bed and rushed out of the house because they were unable to wake her up. They saw that she was pregnant and knew that she and the baby were in trouble.

Everyone was sad and scared, that is everyone except mom. She acted like she didn't care either way.

CHAPTER 68

When the ambulance got Tabatha to the hospital she was in critical condition. The people at the hospital worked on her very fast. They had to stop the bleeding.

Tabatha had to get an emergency C-section so that she and the baby could have a chance of living. The hospital worked on her for hours after they delivered the baby.

Catherine woke up the next day in the hospital a little sore but feeling much better.

The nurse brought the baby into the room to be with her. When she saw the baby, she had such feelings toward him that she could not describe.

All she knew was that it made her feel good.

She held the baby boy real close to her and began rubbing his hair. She thought he was beautiful. She said, "your daddy is going to be so happy to meet you and I think you are going to like him too."

She continued rubbing his hair and kissing on his cheek; she just couldn't help herself.

She thought to herself; what should I call you, what name should I give you?

She said, "let me call your daddy and tell him that you are here and then we can come up with a name for you.

She called John and when he answered his voice made her nervous. He sounded like he was very angry.

She asked him what was wrong.

John said in an angry voice, "I have been calling and calling for days trying to reach you. Where have you been? Why haven't you called me?"

Catherine said, "John, you have to calm down. I am in the hospital. I had the baby.

John became quiet on the phone.

Catherine said, "did you hear me, John? I am in the hospital because I had the baby."

John asked, "are you okay? Is the baby, okay? What hospital are you in? Are you okay?"

Catherine said smiling, "I am fine John, and the baby is okay too. I'm at Michael Reese Hospital. Are you coming to see us?"

John said, "am I coming to see you, what kind of question is that? Didn't I just tell you that I have been trying to reach you? Never mind, I am on my way right now. I love you, Catherine."

Catherine began smiling even harder and told him that she would see him when he got there.

CHAPTER 69

Jermaine woke up the next morning with a massive headache. He had to get 32 stitches in his head from mother bussing it.

The hospital kept him there overnight just to make sure that he would not pass out.

They released him and told him how to take care of the stitches, but he didn't want to hear anything from anybody.

He was still angry, not at mother, but at Catherine.

He took the papers from the nurse and stormed out of the hospital holding his head.

He thought of all kinds of things that he would do to Catherine if he saw her right now. It didn't matter to him that he was hurt, he just wanted to make sure that she was badly hurt.

He walked all the way home from the hospital because they didn't live far from it. When he got home, the first person he so was mother.

He looked at her and didn't say a word.

Mother said, "what the hell are you looking at? Oh, it looks like someone still has a chip on their shoulder. Is that the case?"

Jermaine just stared at her and didn't say a word. He wanted to but he knew better.

Mother said, "is there something you want to get off your chest? Let me know what you are thinking, son. I got some answers for your ass if that's what you need. Tell me, son, tell me what you are thinking."

Jermaine asked if he could just go to his room.

Mother said, "take your crazy ass on, and don't start no more shit with anyone. You hear me?"

Jermaine nodded his head in agreement but knew it was not the truth.

He proceeded to walk down the hall towards his bedroom. He looked in the girls' room to see if Catherine was there but did not see her.

He didn't know about Catherine having the baby, nor did he know about Tabetha being rushed to the hospital.

Jermaine continued walking down the hall holding his head and processing his evil thoughts.

CHAPTER 70

John arrived at the hospital that morning to see Catherine and the baby.

He was extremely nervous for some reason.

He thought to himself; what in the world just happened? I have a baby now! Everything is moving so fast. I'm starting to freak out. No! No! Get yourself together. You got this! You wanted her to be yours, now nothing is going to get in your way. Now I can show Catherine how I can take care of both of them. She will see now.

John's nervousness calmed down after the talk with himself. He went up to the room and as soon as he saw Catherine, everything melted inside him.

When Catherine looked towards the door opening, she saw John standing there smiling. This made her smile.

John walked over to the bed and kissed her on the head.

He said, "it is so good to see you. Are you ok? Do you need anything?"

Catherine smiled saying, "yes and I don't need anything right now. I'm glad you came, you look good.

John smiled even harder. He loved the way she said he looked good.

John said, "thanks, same to you.

They both laughed a bit.

John asked, "was it time for you to have the baby already?"

Catherine's smile left her face.

She responded, "not exactly."

John asked, "so, what happened to make you have the baby so early."

Catherine became a bit nervous. She did not know how John would take hearing that Jermaine had tried to kill her and the baby.

Catherine hesitated to speak while looking down.

John said, what's wrong Catherine?

He grabbed her hand and began holding it.

He said, "what's wrong baby? You are making me nervous.

Catherine looked up at him and said, "if I tell you, you have to promise not to get mad and do anything crazy."

John said, why would I do anything crazy? What happened Catherine?

Catherine took a deep breath. She said, "what I'm about to tell you will rub you the wrong way, but it's really nothing you can do about it.

John said, "what do you mean I can't do nothing about it?

Catherine continued, "what happened to me was pretty messed up. But you can't do anything about it because he's family.

John frowned.

Catherine continued, "John, I still don't want anyone in my family to know about you. If I tell you what happened, you can't do anything about it because of that.

John became angry. He said, look Catherine, if someone did something to you that made you have my baby earlier, you can't stop me from hurting them. Family or not!

Catherine responded in an aggravated voice, "you see, that's what I am talking about. I just told you that I don't want them to know anything about you and you are talking about doing somebody in my family harm.

She began to cry.

John said, "don't cry baby. I'm sorry, but to think of someone harming you and our baby just makes my blood boil.

Catherine said while sniffing, "I understand, but you will cause a lot of grief for me if you let them find out about you."

John responded, "ok, ok, you win. I still don't understand why you don't want them to meet me."

Catherine said, "just like you not wanting me to talk to your dad, I'm asking for the same thing."

John was offended at first, but then buckled down and said, "you are right! We both got some things to do and get over with our families. Whew!

Catherine laughed and offered the baby to him.

When John held the baby, everything that he and Catherine were talking about went right out the window. The baby had him hooked.

Chapter 71

No one in the building knew exactly what was going on with Jermaine, but rumors began surfacing.

There were a few men in the building that real men called suspect. There was a stigma regarding these types of men.

The meaning of that meant that the so-called real men in the building thought the suspect men were a bit fruity (liked other men).

No one in the building wanted to be recognized as being suspect, because a few of them had been beaten close to death.

But there were a few in the building; known and unknown.

Jermain was still consumed with his thoughts about Catherine.

He said to himself; she thinks she's better than everybody. She thinks that her shit don't stink. Everybody keeps falling for her nasty ass. I CAN'T STAND IT! What's wrong with me? How can he fall for her and not me?

Jermaine continued to rub his head while thinking; everybody thinks there is something wrong with me, but ain't nothing wrong with me. They are the ones that are batshit crazy.

I'm tired of everyone falling over her like she's somebody, especially him!

Chapter 72

John left Catherine at the hospital. His mind was going a mile a minute.

He knew he had to find a place to live right away. He did not want Catherine to have to go back home to deal with all that mess. Not with his baby.

John was furious about what happened to Catherine, but he knew he couldn't do anything about it. He knew that she would be really upset with him if he went to her apartment to confront her brother Jermaine.

So, John pushed the anger aside to begin focusing on finding a place before Catherine left the hospital.

John looked for about 3 days for a house or apartment to rent. He kept running into brick walls. It was more difficult than he had imagined.

He went home after looking at one of the apartments, with frustration on his face.

His mother saw him looking in distress and asked what was wrong with him.

John said, "nothing mother, just got a lot on my mind right now."

She said, "let me know what's going on son. Maybe I can help."

John responded, " Naw mother, I am going to have to handle this myself. I have to!"

John's Mother continued, "give me a try, son. You look like you are carrying the world on your shoulders."

John said, "if I tell you, I don't want you to share this with dad. I really don't want to be bothered with that right now."

John's Mother was caught off guard by that statement.

She said, "son, I'm not sure what you are thinking regarding your father. But I will keep this conversation from him for now.

John asked, "what do you mean for now?"

John's Mother responded, "your father knows a lot of people and if it's what I think it is, he may be able to help you with your problem.

Chapter 73

John's Mother continued, "I understand where you are coming from son. That is why I said for now. You never know what's around the corner, and you may need more than my help."

John just sighed with his head down and walked away.

John's Mother walked towards him and grabbed his shoulders.

She said, "I'm here for you son. Please talk to me and let me see if I can help. I won't tell your father, I promise."

John looked up at his mother and said, "thanks! But I just need a minute to rest my mind. I will tell you what's going on after I rest a while."

John's Mother let his shoulders go and just nodded her head in agreement.

John walked to his bedroom and laid down. He was exhausted from looking for somewhere to live.

He knew that he was running out of time because Catherine and the baby were getting out of the hospital soon.

Before he knew it, he was fast asleep.

Chapter 74

Tabetha awoke a few days later from having emergency surgery. Her body hurt like hell.

She looked around the room trying to figure out where she was and what was going on with her body.

A nurse came into the room and said, "good morning sleepy head. You were out for a while lady.

Tabetha's throat was a bit dry. So, she asked the nurse for some water.

The nurse came right over and poured her some water.

She said, "you gave everyone a bit of a scare there, hun."

Tabetha looked at the nurse with a confused look on her face.

The nurse asked, "you don't remember, do you?"

Tabetha shook her head motioning no.

The nurse said, "well honey, you were rushed in here because you were bleeding pretty bad. That's a no, no in this business especially if you're pregnant. You had to have emergency surgery so that you and the baby's life could be saved."

Tabetha was shocked by the news. She tried to remember the event, but she was still a bit groggy.

The nurse said, "it's ok that you don't remember right now. You have been through a lot, but it will come back to your remembrance soon enough sweetie.

Tabetha asked in a soft voice, "what about the baby?"

The nurse responded, "the baby is doing just fine. She's just waiting to meet her mommy.?

Tabetha thought to herself; mommy! Who am I to be someone's mommy? I don't want to be anyone's mommy. What am I going to do?

The nurse continued, "don't worry about anything hon. Rest up and we will get you to your new bundle of joy soon.

Chapter 75

John woke up from his nap and went to the kitchen to get something to eat and drink.

John's mother saw him go into the kitchen. She got up to meet him.

John saw his mother coming filled his cup with water and began to sigh.

John's mother said, "hey son, I hope you slept well.

John continued drinking his water.

John's mother was a bit nervous because she knew that he didn't want to talk about what he was doing. But deep in her heart she knew that she could help him, she just didn't know what kind of help he needed.

John said, "hey mother! Please give me a minute to get something in my stomach.

John's mother said, "sure, sure son. Would you like me to fix you something?"

John responded, "no, I got it. My stomach feels like I haven't eaten in years."

John's mother smiled and walked back into the living room.

John was glad his mother gave him a break. He had to make sure that he was processing everything the right way.

Showing Catherine that he had her back was the most important thing on his agenda.

John wanted to make sure that nothing else bad would happen to her and his son. He would be their protector.

John made himself a couple of sandwiches and went back to his room.

Chapter 76

Tabetha was still a bit groggy from the surgery. She was also trying not to freak out about being a mother.

She never thought about having children, she was just trying to get someone to love her. Nothing in the world made her think about becoming a mother, because of the mother she had.

Tabetha continued with her thoughts; Now what would I be able to teach a child? I don't even like my siblings, so how am I going to like or love a child?

Tabetha's head began to hurt from the frustration of thinking. She turned over to her other side and tried going back to sleep.

No one knows what the future holds. But Catherine and Tabetha both have to go home.

Which home, who knows?

What progress did John make?

And what does Jermaine have waiting for Catherine?

It's a lot going on, but the future will complete the story.

Made in the USA
Columbia, SC
09 January 2025